ALSO BY ZACH FORTIER

NON-FICTION
CurbChek
Street Creds
CurbChek Reload
The CurbChek Collection
Hero to Zero
Landed on Black

BIOGRAPHY
I Am Raymond Washington

FICTION

The Director Series: Baroota: The Hunting Ground
Cachibaché
Izadi
Chakana

SCIENCE FICTION
The Overseer Series
Volk

 Scan the QR Code to the left to
purchase Zach's other books.

BAROOTA:
THE HUNTING GROUND

ZACH FORTIER

BAROOTA THE HUNTING GROUND

Published by
SteeleShark Press

ISBN-13: 978-0692651544
ISBN-10: 0692651543

Visit the author at:
Website: *www.zachfortier.com*
Blog: *www.authorzachfortier.blogspot.com*
Facebook: *www.facebook.com/authorzach.fortier*
Twitter: *www.twitter.com/zachfortier1*
Goodreads: *www.goodreads.com/author/show/5164780.Zach_Fortier*
Instagram: *http://www.imgrum.org/user/zachfortier/505378433*

BAROOTA:

A WORD WITH ABORIGINAL ROOTS MEANING "HUNTING GROUND"

"To die proudly when it is no longer possible to live proudly. Death freely chosen, death at the right time, brightly and cheerfully accomplished amid children and witnesses: then a real farewell is still possible."

~*Nietzsche*, Twilight of the Idols

CHAPTER 1

"Just pulled up outside," Nick texted as he arrived in the parking lot.

Texting while driving on post is a federal offense these days, so he waited until no one was looking. The military is so uptight now; nothing like when he was in, but those were different times.

As Nick pulled into the crowded parking lot, people walked down the sidewalks in an orderly fashion, "brainwashed maggots" he would have called them back when nuclear war was the main threat and no one had ever heard of the Taliban or ISIL. The conformity was nauseating to watch, but part of the lifestyle, Nick supposed, and one of the huge reasons he got out when his time was up. It amazed him now looking back that he was able to survive the time he'd spent in green – and actually, truth be told, not only did he survive, he'd thrived, but it wasn't always an easy gig.

The phone vibrated in his hand, and he checked to see JoAnn's reply, "OMW" light up the screen on the smartphone; it was their code for, "On My Way". In his mind, Nick could see her entering the elevator and smiling as the doors closed.

He thought back to the last time they were here for her work… it wasn't a pleasant trip. He watched the crowds of people leaving the building now with a whole other agenda, looking at rank insignias, checking nametags. If Nick saw the motherfucker, it was on. The asshole would remember this day for the rest of his life. No matter how much he looked – and even when he showed up unannounced, scanning – Nick could never find him. That memory still flashed white hot in his mind.

Nick could feel his back and chest tightening as the memories flooded back into his now blurred vision. He noticed the death grip he had on the steering wheel and tried to relax. It was six months ago when he found the texts on her phone, six months of daily searching for reasons to stay in this relationship. In the end, Nick stayed, hoping to rebuild and perhaps move on, if that's ever possible after such a betrayal. Now it was day by day; back then it was minute by minute.

Nick saw her leave the building as she swung open the double glass doors and walked down the sidewalk to where he'd parked. Still, he watched for any sign of anything amiss or unusual…six months, and it felt like yesterday. White hot rage started to boil up, and Nick thought, *I have to calm myself.* Breathing deeply, he talked in a low tone as the rental car's air conditioner blew cold air on his face.

"Chill, man, chill. Save it for when he finally slips and makes his face known."

As Nick got out and opened the passenger side door as she approached the car, a female captain walked past and commented, "What a gentleman he is."

Nick didn't respond; JoAnn, however, replied to the captain, "Yes, he is! Aren't I lucky?" while flashing a bright smile for all to see.

Inside, thinking in a Sam Kinison-like scream, Nick spewed venom as he heard Sam's voice in his head, *Yes, you are very lucky – lucky my ass is still here at all.*

However, Nick said nothing and smiled as he closed her door. As he got in the driver's side, she reached over, kissed him, and said, "How was your day? Did you work out this morning?"

Watching the men walking past, still looking for "Daddy", as she called him, Nick was vaguely aware that he answered her, something about, "Yeah, I had a good day, and the workout felt good today."

He slowly pulled out of the parking lot, watching everyone, scanning mirrors, looking for some smirk or gesture that would draw his attention to the now walking dead man. There was none.

Nick thought, *Man I really need to calm down. Seriously, I need to chill. There's been no sign of anything going on for months now, time to move on. Enjoy today, and let bygones be bygones. Everyone makes mistakes, let it go.*

He started to relax, then in the darkest, deepest corners of his mind he heard a dark, evil voice; no, not really a voice, more like a thought that has a life, a mind, a will and a laugh of its own say, *That will never happen! Never!*

Somehow they'd left the main gate, and Nick was now suddenly aware that she was telling him about her day; something about meetings, and sending out reports to the brass. She worked as a contractor, working as an IT consultant for the government. Most of what she said, Nick had known nothing about. They came from different worlds; well, maybe not so different at the beginning, but they were in different worlds now. As children they both had hard lives, and that was their common ground now. Nick dealt with it by his stubborn refusal to give in to anyone; she dealt with it by using her sheer, raw intelligence. You won't meet a more intelligent person in your lifetime. Their past, however, had left its mark. They joke that they're damaged goods, and it was true. Damaged and like-minded, soul mates…or at least he'd thought.

Anyway, she told him if he was up for it, they'd been invited to dinner with one of her co-workers, Jessica.

Nick asked, "Where does she want to go?"

JoAnn said, "The Mashhouse."

He mulled it over in his head for a minute and then finally said, "Sure."

He liked The Mashhouse; they had amazing blondes, and the food was OK, too. By blondes he meant the beer, not the waitresses. The Mashhouse was a micro brew, and the beer they call blonde was usually one of the better brews you could ever hope to drink.

JoAnn said, "Oh, by the way, Jessica will be bringing her boyfriend. I guess she's pretty serious about this one, and she wants us to meet him."

"OK," Nick replied, "What's his name?"

She said, "Jay, I think, and I guess he was in the Air Force but did his time in MI (military intelligence). Now he's here at Ft. Bragg."

Nick grimaced, thinking, *Great, some lifer maggot that's gonna talk all about his last duty station and how he's been all over the world and seen it all and yet can barely tie his own shoes without a tech order to explain how to do it.*

But he said nothing like that and simply replied, "Sure, that would be fun to meet him."

JoAnn smiled and said, "Great, we'll meet them at 6:30. I thought we could go earlier if you'd like, just so we can catch up and talk with each other."

He had to admit, she was trying to make amends…maybe too hard. His life has made him suspicious of everyone, and with good reason.

They arrived at the hotel and parked in the parking lot. They'd stayed there many times, and it felt like their home away from home. Walking into the lobby of the Home 2 Suites, JoAnn turned to him and smiled as she said just loud enough for two nearby patrons to hear, "I was thinking I'd make you my bitch before we go out to eat tonight. Are you up for that?"

It wasn't a request. The thought made Nick's head swim and his eyes grow heavy as he smiled back at her and said, "You're the boss!"

And she was…very much so now. Before the texting bullshit began, JoAnn was very much a woman who needed to be told what to do and when. Now she took charge, and Nick very much approved.

CHAPTER 2

The Mashhouse was just down the street from the Home 2 Suites in Fayetteville, so they left at 6 pm and were there moments later. The place was one of Nick's favorites on their semi-annual trips to North Carolina. Opening the large, heavy wooden doors for JoAnn, they walked into the dark interior. The hostess asked if they wanted to be seated in the restaurant or the bar, and Nick chose the bar area, which was their usual. There were a couple televisions that usually played whatever sporting event was currently being broadcast, and tonight it was the Panthers game. Cam Newton was dancing in the end zone after running in another touchdown. Nick and JoAnn sat in a nook just behind the cashiers' appointed station and ordered two blondes; happily, they found out tonight the blondes were blended with blueberries. They added an order of calamari. The beer and food arrived a few minutes later, and they clinked glasses before diving into the food. The bar side was noisy, so talking required more effort than usual. Nick and JoAnn people watched and made comments to each other about the other patrons' social oddities while they ate and waited for Jessica and her new beau to arrive.

Finally, Jessica arrived and introductions commenced. She introduced her boyfriend as Jay and then motioned to Nick and said, "That's Nick, and this is JoAnn."

Jay laughed and said to Nick, "So you're the odd man out, huh?"

Nick asked, "What do you mean?"

Instantly, the rage began to boil to the surface. Nick thought he was about the knock Jay's teeth out at the first smirking comment about JoAnn's past indiscretions. Jay must have sensed Nick was in no mood and quickly explained how Nick was the only person at the table whose name didn't start with the letter "J".

Nick studied his face for a minute and decided Jay's answer was honest, and possibly truthful. The group was quiet and, he noticed, uncomfortable with his intensity. So, Nick laughed and said, "Yeah, I guess you're right. All three of you are 'J's".

The meal began with Jessica and Jay asking how the blonde was tonight and sharing the remainder of the calamari with Nick and JoAnn. Jessica was an outgoing, gregarious woman who swore like a sailor and had a toxic and funny sense of humor. They'd had dinner with her before, and she was always fun to meet with and talk to. Jay was much like Nick and spoke very little, whereas the two female co-workers immediately dove into the latest gossip from work.

Finally, Nick asked Jay what he did for work. Jay carefully responded. Nick noticed as Jay spoke that every word was carefully thought about and weighed for accuracy. He didn't speak lightly or off the cuff; the cadence of his speech was deliberate and measured. It was notable and immediately odd at the same time. His carefully measured speech took time, much more time than normal speech would, and Nick had to listen intently to make sure he didn't miss a thing over the loud crowd responding to yet another touchdown.

Jay was retired from the Air Force and was indeed in intelligence. He was now a civilian and worked on Ft. Bragg as a government employee. Nick and Jay talked about places they'd been stationed, what years they were in the military, and finally Jay asked what Nick did now.

"Not much," Nick replied. "Been a cop for most of my adult life, worked all kinds of assignments, and now I'm out. I needed to get out," he explained.

Jay looked at Nick carefully and began to ask questions. "Were you ever on SWAT?"

"Ya," Nick replied, "two different teams, worked entry teams in both."

"Do you still shoot occasionally?" Jay asked.

Nick replied, "I do. It's hard to let go of a skill set that kept you alive for so long. For that matter, I still work out as well, heavy and hard, although my body will never reach the levels it had when I was in my 20s and 30s."

Jay asked for Nick's personal best for the mile.

Nick laughed. "Four-thirty back in the day, back to back in a four-mile race."

Jay's eyes opened wide. "You ran four miles in 18 minutes?"

Chuckling, Nick said, "Yeah, a long time ago. I was on a combat competition team, and we were relieved from duty to compete against the entire command."

Jay smiled. "Wow, that must have been cool. So tell me about your career as a cop."

Nick brushed it out in broad strokes, and he noticed Jay listened intently now and how the careful cadence of his speech disappeared when he asked questions. Finally, Nick asked about Jay's job and career; silence followed, and then the measured speech pattern returned. Nick made a mental note, "Maxwell Smart" is hiding something, and he wondered what it was. Finally, the dinner arrived and they settled in to eat.

Jay explained he liked to run the 'Tough Mudder" races to test himself now and asked if Nick had ever run them.

"I haven't. Not real interested in a contest like that, for no real purpose other than to finish. Reminds me of the running fad in the '80s where everyone had to run a marathon to be legit. Never mattered how fast, just run a marathon and you were a legit runner," Nick explained.

Jay's eyes narrowed, and the quick and more normal pattern of speech returned. "So you like to have a personal goal, a speed to meet, or a max weight to push?" he asked Nick.

Nick replied, "Yes, to just finish was never enough."

Jay nodded and looked out over the crowd excruciatingly slowly while he formed his next sentence. "How do you feel about women and children being kidnapped and forced into slavery overseas?"

Nick's first thought was, *What an odd fucking question, how do I feel?* So he asked Jay, "What do you mean how do I feel? Dude, that's an odd question."

Jay put down his fork and picked up his napkin, carefully wiping his mouth. His measured movements set off red flags in the back of Nick's mind. He'd seen this kind of measured control before on the streets, usually from a person who had an explosive temper. Nick took a big breath, relaxing, then he took his hands out of his jacket pockets to be ready for anything as he waited to see what Jay would do next. Awkward moments ticked past, and finally Jay responded.

"I'm forming a team for a wealthy benefactor who I call the Director. He wishes to make an impact where the government cannot or will not. This person wants to make a difference when it comes to women and children being kidnapped and sold into sexual slavery worldwide. This person wants to remain anonymous and wishes to work off the books with the State Department and conduct rescue missions. The work isn't government sanctioned, but also not interfered with by the government. If we're caught, we're on our own." Then another cautious, measured pause as Jay looked out over the bar in a dramatic, measured sweep, which finally came full circle back to meet Nick's gaze. "Would you be interested in being on that team?"

Nick leaned back in his chair and looked at Jay for several minutes without saying a word. He saw Jay thought what he was saying was real.

Is this guy a whack job? Nick ran down in his head all the things wrong with Jay's statements. The government knew about these operations, but didn't interfere? A wealthy benefactor who just wanted to do good, worked with the State Department, but independently funded this operation? And you want me, a 54-year-old burned out cop damaged beyond belief, to join this team based on a conversation we have at dinner? Nick assumed the operation was classified "Secret" at the very least, and "Mr. I-Robot" just spilled it over dinner?

Nick said none of this and instead just continued to run down the list in his head of all that was wrong with this conversation. The list grew and grew, and finally Nick replied, "No. Maybe a few years ago I could and would have been interested, but now I'm just trying to heal from all the damage. Just the thought of children being sold as sexual slaves fires me up. I'm calm now as we sit here eating, but trust me, I can fire up to toxic levels in the blink of an eye. You need stable, calm, tactical people on a team like this, not damaged old fucks like me."

Nick noticed the table had gone quiet as Jessica and JoAnn listened to their exchange.

Jay nodded and said, "I agree, but you'd bring to the team an element I can't train into the military guys I've recruited for this team. You're an independent thinker, and more than that, a critical thinker. You're used to working alone, and you understand the legal aspects of this operation. Your law enforcement background is unusual, at best. You're still fit and shoot, and yes, you may be damaged, but I think everyone on the team is damaged in one way or another."

To Nick this was all bullshit, none of it rang true. He just said again, "No, not interested. My life now is taking care of her and trying to make the best of what life I have left to live."

Jay said, "OK, I get that. Just think about it; if you change your mind, contact me." He pulled out his wallet and removed a card with his work and cell phone numbers on it.

Nick took the card, then they changed the subject, moving on to sports, iPad apps, and technology. Eventually, dinner came to an end. They said goodbye to Jessica by way of a hug, then Nick shook Jay's hand.

Again, Jay said, "Think it over; we have six months to train up for the next mission, and I'd really like for you to be with us. I think you'd find it a rewarding experience."

Nick said he'd think about it, then they parted ways.

JoAnn and Nick walked to the car, and he opened her door. She paused to kiss him as she got into the car. Closing the door, he walk around the car and watched as Jay and Jessica left the parking lot from the other side of the restaurant. They were talking and smiling, and Jay didn't look in Nick's direction at all.

Weird damn dude, Nick thought to himself as he got in the car.

Sleep was hard to come by that evening. Nick thought about the last time he felt like he'd done anything that mattered; it had been a very long time. Folding laundry, making dinner and lifting weights to deal with anxiety was his daily routine now. Nothing he did made a difference. If even just one of these rescue operations was successful and real...he thought long and hard about the training that would be required, physical, mental, tactical. He was nowhere near what he used to be and not sure he could ever return to the razor sharp edge required to make a difference – and more than that, survive an operation like the kind Jay was referring to.

Finally sleep came, filled with fitful and dark visions, full of old memories of long dead faces Nick was never able to eject from his sub-conscious.

The next morning, he made no mention of the conversation with Jay at dinner or the thoughts floating around in his head. He and JoAnn went through the daily routine they always went through on these trips. Nick went to the lobby to get breakfast for the two of them while JoAnn showered and prepared for work. When she was ready, he would drive her to work, drop her off and watch as she walked into the building.

Nick would return to the hotel and begin the workout that would occupy the next two hours of his day. Today was their last full day at Ft. Bragg until the next trip. They'd planned on leaving the next morning for the long flight back to their mountain home.

After dropping JoAnn off, Nick returned to their room and cancelled his workout plans. Opening the laptop, he started to do research on human trafficking, which countries were most involved, which organizations, possible methods used to move and distribute people to potential buyers. How many of the victims were recovered? Not many, Nick found out. No one seemed to care once you hit the black hole of being kidnapped, no one seemed to follow up, or for that matter even know where to begin to follow up. Local police didn't coordinate with federal officials, and when they did, no one took ownership of the cases; the case was handed off, much like a relay race, and then dropped into a bottomless pit of paperwork and red tape.

The animals that did this kind of thing had constitutional rights as well, and like Jay had said, the government had its hands tied by those protected rights; however, a black ops team properly trained, dangerously motivated, and off the books could unleash a medieval ass kicking on these animals.

The idea made his heart pound. He'd been involved with many of what those in law enforcement called "milk carton kid" cases. Children taken from their families or manipulated by predators to go willingly and then disappear into the night, only to reappear several months later married and/or pregnant with their newfound love. They'd have new names, identities and initially be resistant to law enforcement's attempts to extricate them from this twisted relationship. Inevitably, once they realized they were finally and truly safe, they broke down and cried hysterically.

One girl told Nick she couldn't believe no one had recognized her; her face was plastered everywhere, yet the people around her didn't see her. She and her situation were invisible to them. Nick thought at the time, *Welcome to reality. No one really cares, and no one pays any attention to what's going on around them. Sorry, little one, people are really stupid and lulled into a state of gullible unawareness that's really frightening. There's no one coming to save you. The world is a very ugly and messed up place, unless someone steps up and does what needs to be done.*

Nick looked out the window thinking, he would later guess for hours until the cell phone buzzed in his pocket, waking him from this intense, dark train of thought. Looking down, he saw a text message waiting. JoAnn was ready to go to lunch. Nick was numb from not having moved for hours. The idea was intoxicating, to be back in the mix for one last ass kicking hurrah. He had to shake off the idea and return to the real world. It was time for lunch, but the feeling lingered no matter what he did to try and shake it off.

A half hour later, Nick and JoAnn were entering Arby's, their usual lunch spot on these infrequent trips. They ordered from an overly exuberant clerk who Nick thought was either on some kind of anti-depressants or perhaps just found out she won the lottery, but continued to work? He didn't know, but her energy was over the top. He just wanted a sandwich; he didn't want to talk about his day, where he was from, and how many kids he had – he just wanted to eat, OK? She didn't pick up on that, though. He wasn't on Paxil, and not in the mood. So not only was she happy, she was dense and unaware; just his luck.

"Have you heard a word I said?"

"Huh?" Nick said as he snapped back to reality.

"I said, have you heard anything I've said?" JoAnn repeated.

Nick said, "Sorry, I guess not. I'm a little bit preoccupied, sorry. So what were you saying?"

"Never mind, it isn't important. So what has you so preoccupied today?" JoAnn asked.

Nick replied, "Umm, well, you remember the weird question Jay asked me at dinner the other night?"

"Sure," JoAnn said as she displayed an exaggerated stare over the restaurant, mocking Jay's peculiar habit the previous night, except this display was sarcastic and kind of mean. Finally, she too looked Nick right in the eyes and said, "'Do you want to join me in saving the world and ridding it of all evil?' That question? You aren't seriously thinking about that nonsense, are you?"

Who, me? No, why would I? Why would I want to entertain the idea of doing something more than making the bed every day? Washing your clothes, making you breakfast? Why would I turn a blind eye to 1.2 million children kidnapped and sold into sexual slavery every year, most of which are between 10-14 years old? Why would that bother me in the least?

Nick said none of this, but this and much more crossed his mind.

In the end, he finally mumbled, "Yes, I am. Have you ever heard the name Jacob Wetterling?"

JoAnn stated, "No, why should I? Is he important?"

Nick said, "Depends on who you ask. Just listen, don't talk, and don't interrupt. Just listen. OK?"

"Sure," JoAnn said.

Nick started his story. "Jacob Wetterling was the first wanted poster I remember reading as a new cop. I'd just started working, and I was trying to learn everything as fast as I could. Jacob was an 11-year-old kid that went missing a few months after I started at the sheriff's department. He was from Minnesota and went out for a bike ride one day and never returned. I followed the case, actually still do. I never worked it; it was many states away from where I worked, but I felt some kind of weird connection to it. It happened right after I started, and I never forgot about it.

Anyway, years later this woman is dumpster diving in the southern U.S., looking for aluminum cans and anything else she can recycle. She comes across this Polaroid of a woman and a boy tied up and gagged, lying in the back of a van. She turned it in to the cops, and they eventually identified the kid as Jacob, and the girl was actually a woman; she'd gone out for a run in Florida and never returned. The cases were somehow related, obviously. One in Florida, one in Minnesota. This shit angered me deeply, and I never forgot it. There are animals out there hunting people, helpless children and women, waiting for the chance to get away with this kind of shit. This was why I became a cop. I promised myself then, way back then, before we ever met, that if I had the chance, I would do whatever it took to make animals like the people that took those two, Jacob and the woman in the van, make them pay – and pay in blood. I feel like this might be the last chance I'll ever have. I'm old, but not too old. Yes, I'm damaged and broken from all the years on the streets, but I'm not done yet, not by a long shot. So yes, I'm seriously thinking about Jay's offer. Something about it feels wrong as hell, I admit. Red flags are waving like crazy, and Robot is screaming in the back of my head, 'Danger, Will Robinson, danger!', but I don't care. I haven't decided yet if I'll take him up on this, but yes, this hits home for me. I can't just let this slide by."

JoAnn just stared at him silently, saying nothing. Finally, she said, "Wow, I had no idea this still bothered you so deeply. You know what this job has done to you. The toll it's taken. It nearly killed you, and now you want back in?"

Nick replied, "No, I don't want back in. I want to be off the books, off the damn chain, I want to do what I never could back then: end these motherfuckers, take no prisoners, show no mercy. Make damn sure they never hurt another person again. I don't want back in. I want closure for all I could never do. I want payback, eye for an eye. I want these animals to know the fear these two felt tied up in the back of a van, never feeling safety or kindness again."

CHAPTER 3

"Jay Blackfoot, may I help you?"

Hello Jay, this is Nick. We talked about two weeks ago at The Mashhouse, in Fayetteville. We went to dinner with you and Jessica, remember?"

"Yes, I do remember. How are you? I hope you're calling to tell me you're thinking about my offer – or better yet, you're going to join the team."

"I am thinking about it, but I have some questions. First, why me? There are plenty of younger, stronger, and frankly less fucked up people out there who would jump on this opportunity. Why not pick one of them?"

"Well, yes, you're right, there are plenty of others out there who are trained. I'll be honest, we've done a few missions, and the last one didn't end well. We were wiped out, we lost everyone, and after doing a lot of research and debriefing, we came to the conclusion that we were too predictable. Too well trained in what's become routine tactics. We came to the conclusion we needed a wild card. Someone who under-stood the tactics and language, but by their very nature and experience would bring an unpredictable element to the team, a fresh set of eyes and ideas. You would be that intangible element. I don't want you to train with the team until the last possible moment, and then only to get familiar with each other. You'll have to train on your own, firearms, tactics, and fitness, all on you. Done your own way, and separate from the team. If you agree, you'll have to pass tests the last week and show you're proficient and capable. The team leader will have to approve you. That's why I asked you to join the team."

Nick thought about this logic for a moment. He did agree that if you were too predictable in your tactics, it was a weakness that could be easily exploited. He'd seen it many times on the street. Cops who would become too regimented in their approach or tactics would get a rude awakening. If they survived, they learned to become fluid in their thinking or get the hell off the street. The street is too dynamic and dangerous for lazy, sloppy work. It made sense, at least to him. He'd made a career out of seeing things with new eyes and going against the grain.

"Jay, I have one question."

"Sure, shoot."

"Say we're successful and free some of the victims, what are we doing with the rest of the people there, the people who took them and held them?"

There was a long pause, then Jay replied, "Nick, we're off the books for a reason. When we're done with this location, nothing will be left standing, nothing will be moving, walking, breathing or complaining to some congressional committee about some bullshit human rights violation. The victims will be removed and taken to safety, then we'll scorch the earth we found them on, and anyone we find there will cease to exist, if you understand my meaning. The last mission was a failure; we lost every single man on the team, and they died slowly, painfully. This mission is payback, and more than that, a wake up call for the people who killed my last team. We've heard your challenge, and this will be our response. There will be no mercy."

Nick said, "OK, I'm in. When do we go? How much time do I have to prepare?"

"We leave in six months for South America. Start your training, and keep me updated on your progress with weekly reports. Glad to have you aboard. I'll let our director know you've joined the team. I'll notify him as soon as we're finished talking."

"OK, starting today, Jay, hope to make this a success, and maybe make a difference. Talk to you next week."

"Good, talk then. Train hard, 6 months is a short time to prepare."

Nick hung up and started to make a mental list of what he would need to do to prepare.

Hitting the blinking line 2 button, the director said, "Speak!"

Jay replied, "Yes sir, the team is nearly complete; the cop I told you about has just signed on."

"Will he be ready in time?"

"Yes, he will be. He's training on his own, he'll be ready," Jay stated.

"He better be. And the rest of the team, are they assembled and training?"

Jay replied, "Yes, all but the woman. Are you sure you want her on the team? That'll be a hard sell to the rest of these Captain America - Death From Above types."

"I don't care what they think, she's a last-minute addition. I need her there, this is a personal favor asked of me by an old and dear friend. Don't question it. I don't pay you to question me, understand? Get the team together, make it happen. That's your job. I'll take care of the rest. Don't think, Jay, just do!"

Jay abruptly stated, "Yes, sir. Sir, may I ask about the pilot? Do we have that end confirmed?"

The director said, "The pilot is not yet confirmed, nor is the aircraft. We'll be on time, one way or the other. Get the team trained and ready, and I'll inform the others of the timetable. If this works, we'll be wealthy beyond your wildest dreams. Once the word is out that we can deliver the product, the maggots will come crawling out of the woodwork, willing to pay whatever we choose to charge. You will be a wealthy man, Jay, you and the rest of your talent scouts."

The phone went dead. Jay smiled as he slowly hung up the phone.

CHAPTER 4

In South Africa, there exists a barely spoken of type of medicine. It is a dark, toxic medicine. Muti medicine, as it is called, is basically practiced in South Africa in place of real medicine. It is perhaps the reason the locals have such a difficult time understanding how to combat or deal with real diseases like Ebola and AIDS.

Muti medicine is magic, or perhaps better described as the belief that human body parts, preferably taken from a live human, have magical powers when used properly by a gifted medicine man, or witch doctor. Of course, some parts are better than others, holding more magic and more power. Sexual organs, in particular, hold a lot of potential for power if properly harvested from a live victim. And the absolute cream of the crop, crème de le crème of sexual organs, are the organs from an African Albino, or a black person born with naturally red hair. Any witch doctor worth their hoodoo bag of tricks can muster up "big magic" given the sexual organs of a red-headed or albino "black African". It is a well-guarded secret and rarely discussed that these harvests continue today in South Africa.

One of the most widely known incidents of Muti murders is the 2008 Kei Ripper murders. During the investigation, a few of the organ harvesting body part dealers were captured, and some were killed by stoning. One, however, was interrogated by local police and admitted to harvesting the organs of an 11-year-old boy. The man admitted to convincing a group of young boys they could play a game of pretend dying, during which he would harvest their organs, and then they would come back to life. The boys agreed until the man, named Gwayi, actually started to remove their friend's liver, fingers, penis and eyes as he lay dying. They refused to help him any longer, according to his statement to the local police. What the story doesn't add is that the boy, whose name was Vika, had an older sister.

Vika's older sister was named Nõnkos, after a famous prophetess in the mid to late 1800s. Nõnkos and Vika were members of the original Xhosa people in the Butterworth area of South Africa. Nõnkos was to be the next target of the Kei Rippers but escaped with the help of family members. She was given bare essentials for survival and told to leave and never return. Unfortunately for Nõnkos, she was born with the power of red hair and fair skin in the mostly dark-skinned region. She was highly prized as a potential victim to be harvested for witch doctors wanting to get rich and gain additional status for their dark spells. Nõnkos escaped that night and wandered for weeks, starving, dirty and disoriented; she nearly died.

Wandering aimlessly and nearly dead, she was found by a woman who promised her sanctuary and food. The woman was kind and cleaned her up, fed her, dressed her properly and provided a bed for Nõnkos to sleep in. Nõnkos felt the terrors she had known for the past few weeks were finally over. She slept well and would awaken rested, and for the first time in a long time safe. Her sanctuary was a façade, however, as she would soon discover.

One morning she awoke to a man standing over her, looking at her in a way the village men had looked at her as she started to mature into womanhood. There was a hunger in his eyes she understood was madness; the madness of lust and power over another human being. The woman who had been protecting her had sold her to a human trafficker, a person who sells others for slavery, usually sexual slavery, to the highest bidder. Nõnkos had escaped one hell in exchange for another. She was fourteen years old.

Her captor was neither kind nor gentle; she was raped repeatedly for several days by him and others in his group before being finally sold for one hundred American dollars to another trafficker – and then the whole process repeated itself. She had no idea how long she had been held and completely lost track of time. Life held no meaning, the pain was unbelievable, and finally she began to wither. Her will to live was waning, and she was about die – looking forward to it, actually. Hoping for a quick death, she was lying on the dirt floor of her "room" one night when she began to have a vision. Her namesake, the original Nõnkos, visited her in the dream and promised her that if she would fight back and find the courage to rise up against her captors, she, Nõnkos the prophetess, would protect her and guide her for the rest of her life. She only needed to take the power from her most demented tormentor, Prophetess Nõnkos explained, and she would be protected from then on.

Nõnkos awoke from the dream and left her small room in the dead of night. She walked among the camp and found that everyone was asleep, drunk and passed out from the evening's celebration. They had just acquired a new flock of young female sex slaves to sample before they sold them into slavery on the black market. She had no idea, but they had already planned to kill her the next morning. She was damaged goods to them now, older now and used up. She had no worth on the black market. Nõnkos walked the camp, looking for her tormentor, and found him in his mud hut. He was unconscious, and a girl much younger than her lay weeping at his side. She was bleeding from her nose and anus, as she had been anally raped by her captor after being beaten into submission. The girl was startled when Nõnkos entered the dirt hut, and she crawled into a corner whimpering. Nõnkos motioned to the girl to be silent and leave the hut, which she did. Nõnkos bound the man's hands and feet carefully, using the same coarse rope he had used on her and so many other girls as he used them for his sadistic needs. When at least she was sure he was tightly bound and could not escape, she stuffed a rag into his mouth, then as he started to awaken, she hit him hard repeatedly over the head, knocking him nearly unconscious. She then took his power, his screams muffled by the rag in his mouth.

She left him bleeding and powerless, as her namesake had demanded. She then walked into the night, protected and unafraid, and was never seen or heard from again.

SEVEN YEARS LATER...

Nõn sat at the table of her favorite Starbucks, waiting to meet the curious, strange man who had asked for an hour of her time. He said he had a story he thought would interest her and that he'd make it worth her time if she'd just give him an hour of her uninterrupted attention. She was intrigued by the offer and decided it would do no harm to meet. She told him where and when and arrived early, as was her custom, to make sure nothing was amiss. Her cautious ways had diminished some in the past few years, but still she remembered that safety was an illusion. That was a lesson she would never forget.

She came armed with her favorite knife. It was clean and sharp and hand made for her by a strange little man she had met at a craft expo while doing research on one of her earliest writing pieces. He was a self-proclaimed craftsman, his works displayed on a card table. The other tables at the event displayed cross-stitch, quilts, photography pieces and an occasional vegetable display that had painted faces on small squash or pumpkins. No one had stopped at the knife makers' display except her. She stopped and looked at the knives and began asking questions. He promised a knife that was razor sharp and hard, so hard it would cut another knife. She smiled a bright, energetic smile and said, "Show me," with an ever so slight accent lingering in her now near perfect English. He did just that. Picking up a knife he had forged, he asked her to pick from his collection of old kitchen knives. She handed him a rusted old paring knife and said, "Cut this one, and we can do business." The odd man smiled and asked her to step back. He then slammed his knife down hard on the back side of the older rusted knife and severed it completely; not breaking it in half, but cleanly cutting it. Impressed, she described the knife she wanted him to forge. He could name his price, but it had to fit her exact description. She explained to him the knife was special and reminded her of a knife that had been hers many years ago, a knife that held great meaning and symbolism for her. Could he do that?

That knife had become her constant companion, her guardian and protector, and she had named it after her brother. She had never used the knife in battle, but it held great comfort to her to have it and feel its custom handle in her hand. It was not ornate or delicate; like her brother, it was robust and utilitarian. Had he lived longer, he would have approved of its practical design. The knife was her talisman. It brought her strength. Smiling, she remembered her brother's bright eyes and smile. Yes, he would most definitely approve. She remembered again how he used to flip her ears repeatedly with his fingers and call her "elephant ears" in their native tongue. It had hurt her feelings then, but now it was a fond memory.

"Ms. Zia?" She was startled back to present day by a man's voice.

Rising, she shook his hand and replied, "Yes! Good to meet you,

Jay, how are you? Can I get you a coffee?"

"How about I buy? I asked you to meet me, so I should buy; it only seems fair, and after I explain to you why we're here, if you decide not to accept my offer, then it'll be the least I can do to compensate you for your time. Sound fair?"

"Sure, then I will have a Caramel Macchiato Vente, please."

A few minutes later, Jay returned to the table and set two drinks down. He took a deep breath and then began.

"The reason I've asked you to meet with me is first because you have amassed an impressive amount of work in the area of exposing human trafficking, both in the United States and worldwide. I'm forming a team that plans on doing something about that particular issue, and I'd like you to consider writing about our success or failures, should either occur. In the interest of saving us both time, I'll stop right there. If you'd like me to leave now, then I'll do so and never darken your door again. However, if you're interested in the slightest in hearing my proposal, then I would ask you to hear me out. I'll be happy to answer any questions to the best of my ability. If I can't answer them now, then I'll get you an answer as soon as possible. Will you hear me out?"

She felt her breath quicken and surprisingly noticed her hand was firmly grasped on the handle of her protective knife. She could feel the contained rage beginning to simmer in her chest as she stared into his cold, pale blue eyes. Taking a deep, cleansing breath, she picked up her drink and sipped the hot, sweet caramel/coffee mixture.

"I suppose you should call me by my first name, Jay. It is Nõnkos, but you may call me Nõn. It is spelled Nõn, but it is pronounced 'Nyen', like the Japanese Yen, with a silent 'y', is what I tell people anyway. Please, continue with your story," she said with a now noticeable accent.

Three hours later, he finished detailing the operation. "So what do you think, Nõn?" he asked casually.

Her coffee was now long cold, and she had not taken notice of it since that first drink. Her hand was aching, she finally realized, as she had never relaxed the now vise-like grip she held on the knife hidden under her baggy Mexican poncho; woven with the colors of her native Africa, it was both bright and comfortable. Jay sat back and stared at her, waiting for a hint or clue of what her decision would be. Her previously bright smile was gone, as was the sparkle that had been in her eyes when he arrived. The woman sitting before him was now formidable and hard. Her eyes unblinking, her stare unwavering. Her entire demeanor had changed from warm and friendly to decidedly predatory and dangerous. He was surprised to find himself thinking he was now very glad he had agreed to meet her in a public place. As he felt a cold shiver starting to travel through his now uncomfortable body, he had to admit, he could see why the director wanted her on this mission. It took considerable effort to suppress the shiver, hoping not to let on that her stare had affected him. She was no one to be trifled with, that was clear. Her writing was passionate and well researched, but more than her intellect, there was a ferocity he was now realizing she could barely contain when provoked. He hoped he had not provoked her.

Finally she spoke, in a controlled, disconnected and unemotional manner. "I will consider your offer carefully. What is the timetable for my decision?" Her accent was now thick and much harder to understand.

Jay answered, "I need an answer as soon as you can give it to me; our timetable is dependent on intelligence we gather and the team's preparedness to execute the plan."

"I will be in touch," she replied and immediately got up, moving smoothly and controlled, like a cat that had been poised to pounce on its prey but at the last minute changed its mind.

Curious, Jay thought as she got up, he had not noticed her accent when he had spoken to her on the phone, but now it was like he was listening to a different person; strange.

Jay watched her as she left. Briefly, he thought he saw hidden under her colorful poncho her hand tightly gripping the handle of a large, crude knife. Jay made a mental note to add that to her profile. No one had noticed that tidbit, and it could be problematic.

Smiling, he also thought to himself, *Bet the director would shit a brick if he sat here with her for 5 minutes, looking at that soulless, empty gaze. I just sat for three hours and discovered the knife to boot.*

The shudder he had been able to suppress moments before exploded through his body, and he found he could no longer suppress it. Taking a large breath, he gathered himself and picked up the two now cold coffees, dumping them into the nearby garbage can. He left the building, thinking to himself, *God help whoever angers that woman.*

CHAPTER 5

The director watched as people walked past the window of his mirrored office windows. Smiling people unaware of the real world around them. He sighed as he reached for the file on the final piece of the large, intricate masterpiece he had been building these past few months. He hated to speak with the woman again. She was foul, impolite, and beneath him in every way; yet, she had come highly recommended in the dark circles he traveled these days. She was said to be the best "freelance" talent available and would ask no questions about the mission, or the cargo. She lacked any concern about the morality of the mission. Her single goal was to be paid, and paid well, and for that she would deliver. The director looked over her impressive resume, 23 years as a pilot for the government, flying for the Forest Service. Dropping firefighters into hot zones, returning with flame retardant and providing cover for "smoke jumpers" that had gotten themselves in over their heads.

Her reputation in the Forest Service was both courageous and insane. It was whispered she had a death wish, but even "death" wanted nothing to do with her caustic, spiteful personality. In a word, she was a bitch. Capable? Yes. Talented? Definitely, but difficult to say the least. What the Forest Service file did not mention was that on her frequent vacations she flew freelance for the CIA, dropping Special Ops teams into hot zones. These "hot zones" were much different than the fires she flew into during her day job. These were manmade hot zones, areas of political unrest, governments needing to be toppled, dictators in need of an attitude adjustment.

She was an adrenaline junky. She had to find increasingly more challenging missions; the more dangerous, the better. Occasionally, prisoners were brought on board and interrogated in-flight. Most exited the plane before it landed; the interrogators had no need of their prisoners' survival after the painful extraction of information. Early on during one of these missions, she had laughed as she heard one of the interrogators' off-hand comment that "it wasn't the fall that killed them; it was the landing," and that "they just needed to work on their landing." In him she had found her soul mate, which if she had a soul would have been remarkable. She did not. They were a perfect fit. They complemented each other. One Chaos, the other Mayhem. He liked to say she had a black hole for a soul, and he had been the only one who could appreciate that quality. Like disease and death, they walked hand in hand. She had been married before they met and had given birth to several children. One day she walked away from it; no notice, no warning. She sent the kids to school, and her husband went off to work. Smiling, she packed her clothes and walked out the door. In her file it was all described with one sentence, which quoted her directly, "I was not meant to be a parent. I just don't give a shit about raising little fucking brats. I am not capable of nurturing anyone, or anything." It was all in the secret files he had access to. He found the pilot distasteful, but necessary. If she was as dark and soulless as suggested, she was a perfect fit for his operation.

It could be a profitable arrangement if she was as good as he had been told. She just needed to learn to be more respectful of him and his station. She had not yet learned respect. Already, she was five minutes late for their meeting. No call, no explanation; just absent. The soothing tones of Bach's Cello Suites calmed his nerves as it played over the interoffice communication system. If music could be food, he imagined this piece would be dark chocolate and salted caramel from his favorite chocolate shop, a small mom and pop treasure he found in "Havre de Grace" one year earlier while on vacation. Savoring the complementary flavors of the music, he remembered the last woman who was late for an appointment with him was, well…reprimanded in such a way that being late again would never be a concern for her again. He smiled as he thought back on that fond memory. Interesting how quickly someone could be made to realize that manners were important. Manners and respect.

"Sir, your 9 o'clock has arrived," the strained voice of his male secretary announced over the inner office intercom.

He grimaced. Here we go, he thought and then stopped and smiled. *No, I think I'll make her wait a minute and give her a taste of her rudeness.*

"Fine, have her wait. I'll be out in a minute."

"Yes, sir."

Moments later, the door flew open and slammed against the wall as it came to a sudden stop. There in the doorway stood the pilot.

She was exactly as he had remembered her, stocky, square, muscular body, no hint of femininity in that stance. She had short-cropped red hair that looked like it had been cut in a fit of rage with a pair of scissors. Perhaps insight into her mental state? He made a note to check out her psych profile for self-mutilation. She wore no earrings, perfume, or makeup as she walked into his office unannounced and uninvited. He waved off his secretary as he ran in behind her, apologizing loudly for the intrusion. He knew the woman did not have manners. He should not have been surprised at her lack of respect.

"Pat, nice to see you again. Please, have a seat," the director said. He then addressed his secretary. "That will be all, Arthur. Please hold my calls until this meeting is over."

"Yes, sir," Arthur replied and quietly closed the door.

Pat met his stare with a steely gaze that spoke volumes about her opinion of him and his expensive suits.

"May I get you a drink, Pat?" he said.

"Sure, double shot of Laphroaig, neat," she replied.

He smiled a tight and slightly angry smile and asked, "How do you know I have Laphroaig in my bar?"

She responded, "All you fancy three-piece suit pussies have Laphroaig in your bar. Just pour it and let's get down to business."

He stopped briefly, hand tightly gripping the whiskey glass, and took a deep, calming breath. Making a mental note, he thought, *If I ever get a chance to correct her behavior, she'll regret that statement.*

He poured two glasses, double shots in both, and returned to his desk, handing her glass to her; she took the glass with no comment, no thank you. Nothing. To make matters worse, she threw a leg over the arm of her chair, spreading her considerable legs in a most un-lady-like fashion and grimaced as she bore down. *BRRRRRRRRRRRAT!*

"Ahhhhh," she smiled and said, "that was a juicy one, gonna have to change my shorts when I get home. Now where were we?"

Like cancer infecting a previously healthy body, a foul, toxic stench began to creep its way into every corner of his office. He felt like he was about to throw up and started to comment but stopped himself. That would be exactly what she would want, his fancy, well spoken protests.

Instead, he stared back at her and commented, "Still pleasant as ever, I see."

She smiled and lifted her glass towards him. "Cheers!"

As he expected, the negotiation would be a chess match with this foul creature. Even more aggravating, she was an excellent negotiator. She was foul, ill-mannered and a downright disgusting human being. She was also brilliant.

She would provide the plane and exit site for the team. She only had a few non-negotiables. First, she did not want to know anyone on the team's names, or for that matter anything about them at all. She said it made her job much easier to "drop the cargo and go."

"If things go south," she said, "I do not want to know. Period. I fly, I deliver the cargo, and that's it. I don't hold anyone's hand. Are we clear?"

"Yes, we are clear."

"I want five hundred thousand up front, deposited in an offshore account in the Caymans. Once I have confirmation of the deposit, then I am in. No deposit, no deal. The remainder of my fees will be deposited when I drop cargo. Clear?"

"Yes, clear."

"Now what type of landing area are we going to drop the cargo in?"

"The area is remote, in the jungles of Panama. The runway is short and paved. It is cleared and safe, but very remote and bordered by heavy jungle on all sides. It will require a skillful landing and takeoff."

Hmm, she thought. "You'll need a STOL aircraft for that. Do you have the length of the runway?"

"Why does the runway length matter? And what is a STOL aircraft?"

"Because, Mr. Armani suit, I can land a plane almost anywhere, but I can't take off from anywhere. A plane that needs a 3200-foot runway to take off can't take off from a 1500-foot runway. It's basic fucking math, goddamn it! What's the runway length? STOL? Stands for Short Takeoff and Landing. You need an aircraft that's built to do that."

He grimaced; he hated profane language. He opened the file on his desk marked "Baroota" and read the description of the area. Finally, after a few pages of information had been sifted through, he located the runway length.

"Fourteen hundred and fifty feet," he announced. Looking up from the paperwork, he couldn't believe his eyes: the woman was knuckle deep in her right nostril, digging for God knows what. He grimaced again. "Please, madam," he said while handing her a box of tissues.

She removed the snot covered finger and said, "No, thanks," as she removed her now filthy and snot encrusted finger from her nose and inserted the disgusting mass into her mouth. Smiling at him she then removed the now spotlessly clean finger.

His gaze darkened. He hated every moment in this woman's presence. She continued on as if nothing was unusual about her behavior, and for her this was not unusual.

"Jesus, that'll be tight; however, it can be done. The aircraft I would choose is the C-130. It's commonly used and has the necessary STOL profile, and it'll be easy to obtain. I can take care of that. I have access to a 'company aircraft', given I possess enough money to grease the necessary palms. Three hundred thousand should do it. In cash, untraceable numbers."

His eyebrows raised; this was more expensive than he had planned, but within acceptable limits. If everything worked out, the plane would be his when the operation was over. He would own the plane, and the foul, disagreeable pilot. The thought made him smile. Soon enough, he would teach her respect.

"That should be no problem," he replied.

"Finally, what's the route you'd like to take? And when do we begin this cluster fuck of a mission?"

"Before I detail the route, I need to know, do we have a deal?"

"Yeah, sure, we have a deal – provided I get paid exactly what I said, and how I said. You'll have your plane and pilot."

"Now about the route and details – oh yes, there is one small detail I haven't mentioned. The crash site location."

"What the hell do you mean crash site?"

"Let me explain."

"I'm all ears, and another whiskey, huh?" She tipped her glass at him, implying he needed to get up and refill her glass. "Oh, and tell me, do you fuck to this music? It sounds like elephants humping in the zoo. I'm sure it makes your kind of people all hot and bothered. To me, it sounds like elephants swapping bodily fluids."

He sighed deeply and got up to fill their glasses. Hopefully, he thought, the whiskey would perhaps dull his senses. The stench this woman had unleashed on his office still filled the air. Remarkably, it had been 2 hours, and pockets of the poison lingered in unpleasant, hidden, invisible clouds here and there. He would probably have to have the entire office cleaned after this negotiation was complete. He would be most satisfied when this was over and she was firmly in his debt.

He returned to the desk and handed her the glass. He made a mental note to throw these glasses away when she left and the meeting was over. She was filth that could not be washed off, scrubbed off, or removed. The glasses were gone as soon as she was.

"Now about the crash site, what I'm going to tell you will be difficult to understand at first, but when I'm finished, you'll see why your complete confidence and discretion in this aspect of the mission is critical."

He had to admit, the woman was horror beyond measure, but when he was done explaining the more delicate aspects of the mission, she did not flinch a muscle. He understood why she had been so highly recommended. She had a razor sharp understanding of the darker side of this mission, and remarkably, her complete lack of couth was exactly what made her ideal for this mission. She was as evil as she was filthy, and unscrupulous; perhaps, he thought, in her case the qualities went hand in hand.

"So after we land and my part in the mission is complete, how will I get back to the United States?" she asked. She then added, "How will you acquire the spare parts and equipment you'll require for the crash site?"

"We were hoping you would be able to assist us with that. Your recommendation is the C-130 aircraft, then?"

"Yes."

"And you can fly that particular plane, I assume?"

"I've flown it several times, and I'm more than familiar with it."

"Do you know a method in which we would be able to acquire the necessary parts for this mission?"

"I think so. There are 'boneyards' of retired and stored C-130 aircraft. I believe with the necessary incentives, I could acquire the parts you'll need to be successful."

"Boneyards?" he questioned. "I'm sorry, I'm unfamiliar with that term."

She replied, "A boneyard is like a junkyard for aircraft. You can't just have an old aircraft towed by a towing company to a local scrap dealer. Aircraft have to be parked in huge boneyards, usually located in the desert. Oftentimes, older planes like the C-130 are cannibalized for their parts. It's a cheaper alternative to buying new parts, and it keeps the plane flying. I have a friend who can make that happen, no questions asked, and he won't be expensive."

"Good, then I'll leave that particular aspect of the mission in your hands." He continued, "Now back to your return trip; you will meet with a small, privately owned yacht and reenter the United States from the Gulf of Mexico. There should be no issues there."

She rolled her eyes and said, "Oh, for hell's sake, aren't you forgetting the minor detail of a passport stamp? How will I explain that I left the U.S. and then returned from South America and have no passport stamp?"

"The United States Coast Guard does not require passport stamps, provided you haven't landed anywhere. Your ship's captain will be on a personal cruise and understands the ins and outs of small vessel smuggling. When you return, you will be tanned and have spent an amazing time in the Gulf of Mexico. That will be your cover. For small passenger ships, the system is honor-based as far as reporting where you have been. The CBP will be contacted, and he will provide them with the necessary details for your return."

"CBP?"

"Customs and Borders Protection," he replied and then continued thinking, *Does she have no manners at all? All she does is interrupt.* "If you choose to look up the details, you may do so, but trust me, we have done a dry run or two to ensure that we understand the nuances of their system. Our captain and his boat are already registered with the SVRS and have an established history; he is part of the 'Coast Guard's Trusted Traveler' program and has a history of making such trips, so yours will be nothing unusual as a cover story, and no unnecessary attention will be drawn to this trip."

"What the hell is the SVRS? Sounds like a sexually transmitted disease to me," she said and then laughed an obnoxiously loud and awkward laugh.

"SVRS stands for Small Vessel Registration Service. It is used by the Coast Guard to regulate small vessel traffic in the Gulf."

"Sounds like you already have all the details worked out. I look forward to a lucrative and long lasting relationship with you and your people."

"Yes, we hope this will be lucrative for both our interests and yours."

She stood up and reached out her hand to shake his. He shuddered as he touched her skin. She grasped his hand, hers rough and strong, while his was well manicured and soft.

She pulled him closer. "I'm sure I can pull off my part in your little 'mission impossible'. I look forward to seeing the six-digit increase in my account. The aircraft will be ready when I have the necessary monetary incentives for my people."

He was surprised at the relief he felt when she left his office. Using a tissue, he picked up her glass and dropped it in the trash. He then went to the bar and began to vigorously scrub his hands.

"Arthur, come in here," he called out loudly through the open office door.

"Yes, sir." Arthur entered the office and immediately was overwhelmed by the stench.

"Please remove this chair and have my office cleaned immediately! Ensure they understand I want them to remove the foul stench of that…person."

Arthur covered his mouth with a lightly perfumed handkerchief in an attempt to manage the stench that continued to permeate the office.

"Yes, sir, most definitely, sir."

CHAPTER 6

It was five a.m. Eastern Standard Time when the phone rang.

"Mm, hello?"

"Jay, are you up?"

"Yes, sir!" Jay immediately sat straight up in bed.

If there was a military term for being at attention while sitting in bed, Jay was doing it. Twenty-five years of training and psychological conditioning had made their impact on his unconscious mind. Yes, he could still think for himself, but at moments like this he realized he was different than the nineteen-year-old kid who had laughed at military veterans for their nearly automatic response to any authority figure. He vowed back then never to become one of them, and yet here he was at five a.m. sitting at attention in his own bed. The two women curled up together in bed with him never moved a muscle, never even flinched. They were not conditioned, and for some reason he resented that. He felt anger boiling up in his chest at this unintentional acknowledge-ment of his conditioning. He'd become what he most ridiculed, at least parts of him had, he thought as his mind cleared and he focused on the conversation he was having. The old guard never would have given a thought about this mission, neither would they have imagined the cash he was about to rake in if all went according to plan.

Again he said, "Yes, sir, I'm here. How may I help you, sir?"

"Is the team ready?"

"The team is ready, sir. They've completed all aspects of the training and passed their physicals. They're ready, sir."

"And our other two players? Detail their readiness for me. Their sponsors wish to know details on their readiness as well. The wild card, is he fit and ready?"

"Yes, sir. I've flown to Colorado and observed his fitness training and firearms training. He's totally immersed himself in the training regiment he designed. He swims in laps in full sweats and shoes in an

Olympic size swimming pool for hours. Apparently, he got that idea from his younger days. He was on some kind of team in the military that must have had a pretty intense training program. His firearms accuracy is better than anyone else on the team. Honestly, sir, I don't think he'll be an issue as far as preparedness. He's focused to the point of being insane. I can see why he was removed from his position on the streets. He is most definitely mentally damaged. I thought the team had some 'whack jobs', you know, 'death from above' types, but this guy is intense. His sponsor will be pleased, I'm sure."

"Good, and the reporter? She has no training to monitor, really, but tell me, is she ready for the trip?"

"Sir, I'm not sure about this one. It isn't whether she's ready or not. She's different. I can't put my finger on it, but she feels wrong to me. Have you read my report on the first meeting we had?"

"Yes."

"To be honest, she gives me the creeps. She just feels wrong, something's off about her. She can be in the room with you one moment, smiling and happy, and the next minute her eyes are dark and soulless. I mean, there's no one there, nothing. It's like she disappears and something or someone else steps into her body. Her eyes aren't all that change; her voice changes, and this weird accent comes to the front of her speech. It's almost like she's a multiple personality or something. Are you sure she's the one for this mission?"

"Yes, her sponsor was quite clear and asked for her by name. She has a remarkable life history. She is definitely the one for this mission. You will make this happen, Jay. Get over whatever it is that you're feeling. You know what's at stake here."

"Yes, sir. Then again, to answer your question, sir, yes, the team is ready."

"Excellent. Send out the orders to meet at The Lake in three days' time. You will ensure the tactical team arrives as one unit. The other two are to arrive individually, they must never feel a part of the team. Their isolation is a requirement."

"When will the support side of the team arrive?"

"The flight crew will arrive in three days. They can mingle with the tactical team, if they dare. My experience is, these two types of mentalities don't mix well and probably will have nothing to do with each other.

I do not want the wild card and the reporter to mingle with the tactical team unless it cannot be avoided. If it looks like it must happen, then I will trust your judgment. But if we can keep them apart, then do so."

"Understood, sir. What about the replacement parts for the crash site?"

"The parts have been acquired, and not cheaply, I might add. However, they're an investment I must make. The observer will be there as well. She is…well, you can see for yourself who she is when you arrive. If anyone should give you the creeps and make you think something is wrong with them on this mission, it's her. I don't think you'll be able to remove the stain of meeting her for some time.

"Jay, all of the other materials have been taken care of and are waiting for you at The Lake. Mission briefing will begin in ninety-six hours. That gives your team 3 days to arrive and get used to the idea that this is finally going to happen. In one week, you land in Baroota, and the mission begins in earnest."

"Yes, sir, I'll make the arrangements and brief you on the progress."

The line went dead on Jay's end. He looked at the phone and saw the screen said "unknown number". The director left nothing to chance. Jay turned off the phone and looked at the sleeping women next to him. The look on his face was predatory. To be so unaware of what was going on around you was both a gift and a curse, he thought, as he ran his hand up the inside thigh of the closest leg to him, exploring the body it belonged to until finally the sleeping woman remembered her place. She awoke smiling and moaning. She and her friend were an excellent distraction he would be able to indulge in more frequently when this mission was successfully completed.

CHAPTER 7

"The Lake" had been a recovery point during the Cold War for nuclear-armed bombers. It was located in a small, out of the way, unimportant no-name town in Washington state, the idea being that in the event a nuclear war did break out, the bombers would deploy. If they actually succeeded in their mission and deployed the nuclear weapons, they would recover to Moses Lake, Washington. The assumption was that the base of origin would be obliterated in a first wave retaliatory strike. In the early eighties, during the height of the Cold War, an entire wing of nuclear loaded B-52s had been deployed to Moses Lake while their home station runway was being hardened and improved for a heavier nuclear load. The deployment was miserable for the support staff required to protect the nuclear loaded B-52s. Posted in a small town with little or no civilian amenities, the ground forces referred to the deployment as "Moses Hole". Since the site was a recovery point for the ancient aircraft and their crews, the bare bones mission infrastructure and technical requirements had to be met for the military. This meant the runway refueling and maintenance assets would be required to be excellent. Moses Lake has one of the longest civilian operated runways in the United States for this reason. After the Cold War ended, the site was made into a civilian runway.

Today, the United States Forest Service uses the site for fire suppression of the drier eastern parts of Washington and Oregon state. The airport is also now a training facility for heavy jets, both military and civilian, and additionally is used by NASA. Because of the frequent aircraft arrivals and departures from so many different agencies, no one had reason to notice the camouflaged C-130 when it landed. There was nothing remarkable about it as the brief puffs of black smoke erupted from the twenty-six-inch Goodyear tires as they gently kissed the hardened and reinforced concrete runway. The plane arrived on the "04" end of the runway and taxied to the pre-designated parking spot on what had been referred to as the twin Christmas trees by security forces in the nineteen-eighties. This was on the "32" end of the run-way. There, the flight crew was picked up by a white Chevy Tahoe after they had completed their engine shutdown and post-flight checklists. They were transported to a small building, which would house the entire flight team. The aircrew would be on the top floor, while when the tactical team arrived, they would be housed in a hangar, sleeping on cots and in sleeping bags in an abandoned office. It was viewed to be a necessary part of keeping them edgy and mentally hard. The "wild card" and the reporter were to be individually billeted in the same building as the flight crew, but on the main floor. Jay would be taking a room on the second floor, along with Pat. She had been apprised of her role as an observer and the boundaries of what her role would be before the team departed. She had accepted the role with a detached, cold acknowledgement that sent chills up Jay's spine. The director was correct: he felt like he needed a shower after just momentarily being in her presence.

Five hours after the flight crew arrived, another group arrived on the airfield. They walked with a confident swagger as they too exited a pair of white Chevy Tahoes, a third Tahoe followed with their gear. They would be bringing the equipment they were familiar with to avoid any possible malfunctions or accidents. Familiarity was a requirement in combat; you had to know your equipment by its feel and texture. It had to be a part of you, an extension of who you were. Anyone who was watching their activity would have recognized the cockiness of a well-trained and self-assured team. Their exact purpose would have been a mystery, however, with no logos, insignias, or rank visible on their clothing or the vehicles that transported them. This was by design; no one would remember the team a few days later, nor would they be able to recall anything noteworthy. Even the Tahoes were rentals from a local car company. That paper trail would die in the 1s and 0s of the Internet with no trace. The team was comprised of all men, approximately of the same age and physical build. None were much larger than any of the others, and contrary to the Hollywood version of a tactical team, the real thing is made up of athletically gifted men and/or women who are not overly muscular. The real "A-Team" was not full of bodybuilders and muscle necks; instead, it was front to back filled with normal looking, average built men and women who were exceptional in talent and skill sets, not testosterone-pumped freaks who could never fit into the uniform. Each member had been chosen for a reason. Each had been a veteran of several deployments in the military, and all had seen combat in the Middle East. That too was a requirement of the director's many financial sponsors. The team had to be gifted and experienced in combat and hostage extraction operations. They had to be battle tested.

The hour and a half drive to the Colorado Springs airport was uneventful. There was no conversation in the car as they drove. She had made her feelings about this trip clear, she thought it was foolish and had held no quarter when it came to criticizing the entire endeavor. The last few weeks had been a war zone in their home, which had only sharpened his resolve. This was going to happen, he had invested too much to turn back now. The laps in the pool, hours running hills and hitting the weight room.

Nick was not in the best shape of his life; that would take a miracle to achieve at this age. He was, however, in respectable shape. His training regimen had been a throwback to what had worked for him before at a much younger age. Shoulders and hips had been the issue from the start. His hips ached now as he sat in the car, but he said nothing. To admit any weakness now was pointless. She would jump on any admission of not being ready for this "pointless trip into fantasy land", as she had referred to it. Nick pulled into the airport and did not bother with parking. She had made it clear she was not even going to bother going into the passenger terminal. He pulled up to the front door of the small regional airport and stopped the car. Leaving it running, he popped the hatchback, prepared to remove his one small piece of luggage. He had packed light. There was no need to bring a lot of clothes. Jay had explained they would provide him with the necessary gear. Nick had requested only a few specific weapons, and according to Jay, those requirements would be met when he arrived at the lake. Pulling the luggage out of the car, he closed the hatchback and rolled his eyes as he saw her still sitting in the front passenger seat. She was waiting for him to open her door. Old habits, he opened the front passenger door, and she stepped out of the car. She gave him a brief kiss on the cheek and said nothing as she walked around the back of the car and waited for him to open the driver's door. Nick walked to the door and opened it, looking into her eyes. He saw no surrender there whatsoever; this was how they would end this disagreement. No good luck, no mention of staying safe, nada. Just a very clear, unspoken "fuck off" as she closed the door and drove away. He had been here before, seemed like every woman he had ever known had an opinion that they felt had to be valued more than his own, each learned in time that was not the case, and each travelled that long, painful path out the door. *Man, I can pick them*, Nick thought as he walked inside the airport listening to the wheels on his luggage clicking on the manmade divots in the sidewalk. He wondered if she would even bother to pick him up on the return flight, if there was one.

Once inside, he checked the bag and made his way through the security gauntlet. A few moments later, he was sitting at gate number four, waiting for the Alaska Air flight #3497 to arrive. Nick would have to fly to Seattle, and from there to Spokane. Once in Spokane, he would have to take a Greyhound bus the final one hundred and four miles to Moses Lake. There wasn't much public transportation that went to Moses Lake, Nick found out as he tried to book a flight, probably the reason they wanted the mission to start there. He sat watching people in the terminal, thinking about what this one last dive into the mix meant to him. Really, now it did seem like a childish idea. What could he really do at his age? Maybe she was right, but thinking about the last three months, he wouldn't have changed much. Lessons learned in his life had taught him one thing: take the chance, the risk, and don't look back. Life is meant to be lived, not hoarded in a box of old photos of things you had once done. Yesterday is gone forever, tomorrow is a maybe, and today is all that matters. Nick stared at the industrial grade carpet beneath his feet and sighed. Forward, always moving forward was all he had ever known.

Taking the cell phone from his pocket, he sent her a text, "Cya in a week." Pushing send, he waited, hoping for a response; none came.

The soul searching was over, and her decision had been made. The dream was clear in her mind. Smiling, she thought about how here she was, an educated woman, she had seen much in her short life and survived things most people in this country cannot imagine exist. Her educated mind viewed the dream as a foolish talisman, nothing to be paid attention to, much less staking so much value in its content. She smiled as she felt her adult mind protesting this course of action. The superstitious and primitive side of her mind had won the battle, and she was not surprised. Something about that time of her life had ruled the day when decisions like this one were to be made. The strength she had felt when she had listened to her spirit guardian that hard day so many years ago was undeniable. The feeling had lingered for days; she did not remember much of what had happened the night of her escape. It felt like someone else was at the wheel, driving the machine of her body, and she was just along for the ride. Years of therapy had given the experience many names and titles, but no one had felt what she had felt that day. No therapist could understand the raw power that had filled her weakened body where none had existed before, giving her the courage and strength to win the day. There was no explanation; it just was.

That was all that mattered now as well. The dream had been as real and powerful as that moment so many years ago. It too just was what it was. What the dream meant, who knew? She had to trust her path, trust that there was a reason for the images, and when she needed to know what they meant, she would know. The three pyramids in the desert were as clear and detailed as if she had seen the great pyramids of Giza with her own eyes. She had Googled the great pyramids afterward and found out there were actually six pyramids, not just three. Her dream had been clear, there were only three, and she needed to follow the wolf as he wound through them. There are no wolves in the deserts of the Middle East. She had checked just to be sure, but the dream was clear. The wolf waited for her, looking at her with a knowing, intelligent look. She had to admit, closing her eyes, trying to extract every detail from the memory of the dream, the wolf had frightened her. There was no clear feeling of kindness or concern for her as he stared at her. The look was cold and disconnected. The look of a predator who has hunted and been hunted. The intensity of those blue eyes burned as he stared at her, silently waiting for her to follow and making clear he would go no further without her. The moment was filled with anxiety, the air was thick with fear and hatred. She could still smell smoke in her dream, and the unmistakable scent of burning flesh. Shots rang out as bullets struck the ground all around the wolf; regardless, he never flinched or wavered. He waited for her, staring in her direction, almost as if he was unaware of the imminent danger, or perhaps he just did not care; she could not tell which. As soon as she started towards him, the dream ended. She had awakened startled, covered in sweat, and breathing from exertion. Even now, her heart pounded in her chest as she recalled the vivid dream. Yes, she heard the protests her educated mind had made, but the primitive, childlike mind was clear. Follow the wolf. She had made the commitment that if she could, she would. She opened her eyes as she heard her flight number announced overhead. She would wait till the last moment to board. She hated to be confined in closed spaces.

The final call came for her flight, and she reluctantly boarded the aircraft. She would be landing in Seattle several hours from now. The flight was going to be long, and she would use the time to do some final research on the subject of human trafficking. It was different when you knew about it from the inside, had actually lived it. Reading stats and articles could not begin to paint the images she recalled as she read.

Hours later, her flight landed rather abruptly at the Sea/Tac airport. The flight had been smooth and uneventful; the landing, however, was difficult. It reminded her of a comment she had overheard a pilot make in an airport coffee shop in Albuquerque, New Mexico. He remarked that flying was not the difficult part of being a pilot; it was the controlled crash that most called landing. He said, "Think about it," to his companion in this conversation. "Landing is really only maintaining control of a crash. You're going to come down one way or another once you leave the ground; the idea is to come down under some kind of control. Crash skillfully, and you live, people praise you and smile as they leave the plane; crash poorly, and your face is all over CNN the next week and everyone dies." The landing in Albuquerque had been a hard one, something about the mountains and the changing cross-

winds had made it a difficult place for pilots to land. She wondered what
had made today's landing so different. Usually, the pilots were able to
control the "crash" well enough that she was barely aware of the wheels
touching the ground. Today, it felt like the landing gear would surely
collapse, the plane had slammed into the runway so hard.

After the usual weather announcements and reminders not to leave
your property on the plane, the door was opened and people began the
tedious process of exiting the aircraft. As she stood up and began to
make her way up the center aisle, she could hear the woman in front of
her starting to swear under her breath. She was middle-aged, stocky,
and had an attitude about the way she carried herself that made Nõn
uncomfortable. She was reminded of the woman who had sold her into
slavery so long ago. Weird, she thought, to make that association now;
she was barely aware of the woman until a moment ago, and now she
had associated her with a person who had sold her into slavery without
batting an eye. Perhaps all the studying and research had made an impact on her mindset more than she wanted to admit.

As the middle-aged woman approached the pilot who was wishing
everyone a good day, she boiled over with rage. "What kind of fucking
landing was that, Junior? First time you ever landed an airplane while
the stewardess was sucking your cock? Jesus, that was a piss poor landing."

The pilot said nothing as the angry female passenger left the plane.
His face was now crimson red, as he was notably uncomfortable by the
angry woman's remarks. Nõn was the next passenger to leave the plane
and told him to have a good day.

He replied, "Thank you, and you as well." No point in making him
feel worse than the angry woman already had.

CHAPTER 8

Nõn entered the Sea/Tac airport with a two and a half hour layover to burn. She headed towards the nearest restrooms. The angry middle-aged woman had the same idea, and they walked in as they blended in with the never-ending crowd of people in the terminal. She avoided the angry woman as they entered the restroom. Just being near her made Nõn uncomfortable. She carried herself with a barely controlled rage, and being near her made Nõn feel as if she had to be ready for anything. Violence rolled off her in wave after dark wave. Instinctively, the other women in the restroom parted as the angry woman split the crowd and headed towards the first open stall. Moments later, the occupants of the restroom had an experience they wouldn't forget for some time.

To most men, the restroom experience is one in which no one says much; you enter in silence, speak to no one, and take care of business. Eye contact and small talk with strangers are forbidden. These are well known rules every male has been socialized to adhere to. A woman's restroom is another world that would make most men cringe in horror to participate in. Women talk and share everything while they take care of their bodies' needs. Some laugh like small children as they evacuate their bowels, passing remarks back and forth from stall to stall. It's the one place women drop the façade of being refined, having culture and manners. In short, women bust ass like nobody's business. The middle-aged woman was about to take this secret feminine folkway to an entirely new level.

As she began to evacuate her bowels, the stench was unimaginable. Giggling, she loudly called out, "Nothing like a vigorous round of anal sex to loosen up the bowels, aye girls?" This was the first of many disgusting comments coming from the now defiled stall. Several women immediately left the restroom, horrified at the scene, comments and smell. Nõn stood her ground, however, refusing to be intimidated by anyone, for any reason. When the middle-aged woman finally did exit her stall, the restroom had been cleared, much to her satisfaction, except for one redheaded black woman.

The middle-aged woman smiled and said out loud, "Where did y'all run off to? I was just getting started," as she waved her arms around in a drunk-like strut. Nõn ignored her and continued to wash her hands, watching as the woman strutted around the restroom like an MMA competitor who had just defeated their opponent in record time. Their eyes locked in the mirror as Nõn watched her reflection. In that moment, she knew the woman was a killer; she could see it in her eyes, behind the victorious smile the woman wore because of her disgusting accomplishment. Nõn recognized evil lurking barely hidden, barely contained. She knew this woman embodied evil; there was no hiding it after they locked eyes. The two women glared at each other, and finally the middle-aged woman broke the gaze and smiled. As she walked up to the sink next to Nõn and started to vigorously wash her hands, splashing soap and water beyond her sink and into Nõn's sink, she began to recite a poem, her voice echoing in the now nearly empty restroom.

"Mr. Garcia went to Taco Bell,
And soon he would experience a watery hell.
He ate a burrito with refried beans,
Then runs to the restroom and pulls down his jeans.
Poot, poot, pooot as gas is released.
It's rest in peace for that toilet seat."

She laughed and laughed after she had finished the poem, and standing back from the sink, she shook off her hands in the air. Finally, she flicked her fingers at Nõn; the last drops of water landed on Nõn's face and shirt, and the stranger said, "Farewell and adieu, my pretty. Hope you enjoyed the show."

Nõn watched as the woman left the restroom, saying nothing. Shaking her head, she wiped off her face. Slowly, women began to trickle back into the restroom, each complaining about the now nearly toxic level of methane wafting in the air.

Nick watched from his seat in the Africa Lounge as women began to pour out of the women's restroom. Laughing, he watched their faces, twisted and contorted, emphasizing the horrors they had been witness to. Smiling to himself, he thought, *I guess someone had a bad flight.*

Moments later, a middle-aged woman walked through the doorway, her face unemotional. Slowly, women began to trickle into the restroom. Nick said under his breath, as the stern woman walked away with a no nonsense demeanor, "And the winner is the redhead bitch." Raising his eyebrows, he wondered what had happened in the restroom to make so many people come shuffling out so quickly. Then he thought better of the idea, better not to wonder. Some things need not be known; let it be.

Moments later, an athletic, red headed black woman walked out of the restroom. She stopped and looked around, scanning the surroundings. To anyone else, the scan looked normal; the woman was orienting herself to the terminal, looking for a hint of which direction held the most promising fast food outlets. Nick, however, saw something different. His survival had depended on seeing what others missed in the most harmless of details. As she appeared to be scanning the terminal, he noticed she always looked at people's hands, and then eyes, quickly moving from one person to another; anyone who was nearby received the quick cursory scan, and when she was satisfied, she moved on. Nick recognized this as a scan for a threat, not a whimsical scan for attractive mates or sexual partners. He watched carefully as she finally and noticeably relaxed, having determined all was safe for the moment. Now the search for a place to eat commenced. She too decided on the African Lounge and walked through the heavy traffic, weaving in and out expertly while never breaking stride.

The sign said wait to be seated, so she waited, and finally a waitress walked up to her and asked, "Will this be for one?"

Nōn replied, "Yes."

"For dinner, or just a drink?"

"Dinner, I think, thank you."

The waitress seated her just behind Nick, at a small table. He would not be able to observe her again without being obvious. So, he amused himself by watching the other patrons of the terminal as they hurried past. Finally, finishing the last of his favorite Aussie Shiraz, Nick got up and gathered his jacket, pulled some money out of his wallet to leave as a tip, and turned to see what the red headed black woman was doing. She was watching him as well. Neither looked away. She was eating some African dish he would never have dared to try. Her comfort level with the strange food was telling. She was probably from Africa, he guessed, or maybe one of those wannabe Africans who had never been to the continent but heavily identified with it, thinking it was their homeland, until Ancestory.com informed them they were from somewhere else. Scotland, maybe? He didn't smile, but the idea amused him. She didn't smile either, and dropped her fork.

Ha! He still had the mojo, he thought as he smirked and turned to walk away. Poker players would call that slip a "tell"; she forgot about her fork as they stared at each other and dropped it. It had been a long time since a woman had noticed him, hell, even noticed he was alive. JoAnn was ass deep in her career and had little time for his emotional needs or issues. Since he'd announced his decision to commit to this mission, she was cooler than ever before. Maybe the workouts had changed his appearance more than he'd realized. Too bad this woman was so young, and in an airport. Too young, really, no happy ending here. He walked off.

Nõn was enjoying the food that allegedly had been based in African recipes. It was not, but it was as close as she'd eaten in years. As she enjoyed the anonymity of sitting alone in the airport, she thought about the dream again, trying to push it out of her mind. She looked up and saw that a middle-aged man was staring at her. There was nothing remarkable about him; dark clothing, greying short cropped hair. He stared back, unflinching; she was vaguely aware that he was exceptionally fit for his age and not particularly attractive. His gaze never wavered, and then momentarily the image flipped. She was staring at the wolf, standing in the desert, surrounded by the three pyramids. The image stunned her like a painful flashback she'd years earlier. She was no longer in the restaurant. She was in the desert. Smelling the burning flesh, hearing the gunshots ripping through smoky air. Stunned, she flinched and her fork dropped, and just as quick as the image had appeared, it was gone. The man was walking away, off into the crowded terminal.

The waitress strolled casually past and asked if she needed anything else. Stunned, she replied, "Yes, I think I'll try the Rooibos tea, please."

"Yes, ma'am, right away."

"And a new fork. I seem to have dropped mine."

"Of course, ma'am."

"Thank you."

"You're welcome."

The tea reminded her of her native South Africa, and was a native favorite. She had thought to ask for the customary curdled milk that was added to the tea when she was a child but then changed her mind. She just held the warm cup in her hand and enjoyed its crude dark aroma. About a half hour later, she heard the first call for her flight. This old habit died hard; she wouldn't leave the restaurant until the final call was announced for her flight. A few short minutes later, she heard, "Final call for flight Alaska flight 416 for Spokane, Washington, boarding at gate number five." Nõn got up and left a tip, paid her bill and walked toward the gate..

Nõn walked alone down the concourse, her feet lightly echoing on the prefabricated flooring as her weight caused the temporary walkway to shift slightly back and forth. The male steward greeted her at the door and closed it behind her as she walked onto the plane. Finding her seat, she was glad to have an aisle seat this flight. It would be easier to depart the plane once she arrived in Spokane. She scanned the crowd, looking for anyone she might know, or anything she needed to be aware of. She saw neither. She relaxed and sat down, buckling her seatbelt and settling in for the short flight.

Sitting in the back of the plane, Nick watched as the redheaded black woman boarded the plane. She liked to be last, apparently, and late as well. He was not impressed. Being late was a pet peeve. Too many years of cleaning up other people's shit storms had made him anally punctual. He had to admit, on time was late in his mind, late was unforgivable. He didn't like late people. Screw them. The fantasy she'd been a few moments later was gone. She probably didn't bathe either. Late and filthy, bad combo. He looked out the window. Focus on the upcoming mission. That was what he should be mentally locked onto, like a hellfire missile.

Approximately an hour later, the plane landed in Spokane. This landing was nothing like the landing she'd experienced in Seattle. Smiling, she quietly whispered to herself, "Excellent controlled crash."

CHAPTER 9

Departing the plane, Nõn walked through the much smaller Spokane airport to carousel number two and waited for her luggage to appear. Behind her, Nick walked quietly at a comfortable distance, watching her. He had to admit, she did have a nice ass. Easy thing to do at her age, no real work required to keep it smoking hot; genetics would carry you a long way if you were lucky enough and didn't eat everything in sight.

While she waited for the luggage, he walked to the Greyhound bus kiosk and paid for a seat on the next available bus to Moses Lake Washington. The bus would be leaving in an hour. The ticket was twenty-eight dollars.

He paid the fee and asked how long the trip would be.

"About two and a half hours, depending on traffic," he was told.

He replied, "Fine, that works. Thanks."

After her luggage erupted through the heavy black plastic curtain that separated the inner workings of the airport from the comfortable façade maintained for the customers, she waited for it to come to her. Reaching down, she picked it up off the conveyer and removed it. Extending the handle, she turned and began to walk to the Greyhound kiosk. Momentarily, she stopped mid-stride; there was the man from the African restaurant. No weird flipping flashback moment occurred this time as she watched. Her initial thought was, *Who is this man? Is he following me? This is too much of a coincidence*, she knew that. Life had taught her well there are no coincidences. He was here for a reason. She thought it better to wait and watch as he bought his ticket, and she walked to a nearby concrete post and stood at its edge, watching and assessing him.

As he paid for the ticket, he suddenly was filled with anxiety; the panic attacks had been frequent lately. He was back in the mix, and this shit had been part of it as well. Living on the edge, training your mind and body to be ready for anything had caused the demons of his past to awaken with glee. Cheerfully, the nightmares had returned to torment him, eviscerated bodies, children burned like they'd been roasted on a spit over a family barbeque, women beaten and mutilated at a rapist's whim, their only crime being lonely and needing to be needed. The floodgates had opened, and all of it had returned. Nick knew that this too was part of being sharp. He needed these memories to remind him that where he had been and where he was now going were no joke. This wasn't a digital representation of what happened in the real world. There would be no director to yell, "Cut and save" when the scene was finally correct. There were no second chances, no second takes to get the perfect lighting.

He instinctively reached for his gun, the conditioned response to reach for the holster well ingrained in his mind. He turned to scan the area around him and saw nothing, no threat. Still, he knew something had queued his anxiety. Looking, scanning back and forth, searching for any sign of a threat. There was none.

The clerk looked at him apprehensively. "Is everything all right?"

He didn't answer. He was too busy scanning, searching. He already knew the clerk was no threat. He didn't waste time or energy trying to make her "daywalker ass" feel comfortable.

Nõn saw the quickened pace of his breathing and the sharp, snake-like strike of his right hand as it snapped up, grabbing for an object at his waist that wasn't there. She instinctively and quickly hid behind the concrete pillar, then began to count to ten. When she reached the magic number, she looked carefully around the opposite side of the pillar and saw he was gone. Searching the area, she saw he was walking to the luggage carousel. He'd been aware someone was watching him; that told her a lot. His movement now as she watched him walk was smooth and fluid. He had either been hunted or had been a hunter. Perhaps both; either way, he was dangerous. She walked to the Greyhound kiosk and bought her own ticket, never thinking to ask about the destination of the man who had been here before her.

A half hour later, the large silver bus arrived and the driver departed, taking a quick break to stretch and get a drink before the final leg of his assigned route; tomorrow he would do the whole thing again, reversed. It wasn't the best job he'd ever worked, but he liked being left alone, and this job provided that. He just drove people to their destinations. He didn't have to interact with them. Other passengers left the bus, and they too took time to stretch and get some air.

Finally, the time had come to get on the bus. Five passengers walked up the metal stairs and began to look for a seat which they would feel comfortable in. Unknown to the rest of the passengers, two of them were carefully and strategically planning for a fight to the death. There were too many coincidences now to be ignored. Calmly, they each took a seat and ignored the other's cautious gaze. The next two hours would be tense for both of them. Neither would sleep.

Going through a checklist in his head, Nick thought about where he first remembered seeing the redheaded woman. There was nothing until the airport restroom. He was sure of that. Her red hair was noteworthy and would have stuck out in his mind.

She was following him; that was obvious. She was fit as well, and a quick visual check revealed no obvious weapons around her waist or hidden in her bags. If she was armed, it would be subtle. Maybe a knife or modified shiv. He'd sit back and watch, let her leave the bus first so she wasn't behind him.

Nõn sat and immediately reached into her bag and retrieved the large ballpoint pen she'd kept there. It wasn't a knife, but it would do in a pinch. The pen was oversized and metal and had passed through many TSA inspections with ease. No one realized how deadly a simple ballpoint pen could be in a fight. It just never occurred to them.

An hour later, it occurred to him, what if they were here for the same reason? Wasn't that the most likely explanation? He closed his eyes and thought about every detail, the food, the restaurant, the type of restaurant, her hair, the refusal to look away as he stared at her. Obviously, she'd been watching him, too. Her body language was now tense, yet fluid like a fighter who had just entered the ring. Loose and explosive, that was how he would describe her movements now.

Then it came to him, in his research into Muti medicine, it had been mentioned that redheaded blacks were coveted for their magical powers. Sexual organs harvested from an "albino black female," as they were referred to in South Africa, had tremendous power. He Googled "authors and Muti medicine" on his smartphone and started to read. Finally, after 30 minutes of searching, he found an article that mentioned the author's name. Nõnkos Zia. Searching the name, he finally found a picture of the author. There she was, his stalker, in color on his smartphone. He read a quick bio of her life, and that told him everything he needed to know. Smiling now, he got up and walked down the aisle to introduce himself. Hopefully, she wouldn't attack him before he cleared the way between them.

She could hear him coming up the aisle and readied herself. The attack would be quick and violent; she knew this from experience. Whoever this now walking dead man was, she didn't care; he'd picked the wrong woman to attack. That would be made very clear to him in a few violent moments.

He sat quickly and slid his arm around her shoulders as he grabbed her right hand with his own. He felt it was safe to assume she had whatever weapon she carried was in that hand, closest to her enemy; quicker strike that way. In one quick movement, they were now locked in a quiet power struggle, each pushing against the other. In a physical life and death chess match, it was a draw.

Smiling, he stated, "You're Nõnkos Zia, am I right?" Her eyes were cold and dark as she glared back at him, saying nothing. Her fury was nearly uncontrollable. "Easy, girl, I'm no threat to you. Listen to me, OK? Please?"

She said nothing; the pressure of her wrist against his hand was matched by his own. She wouldn't allow herself to be victimized. She may not win this fight, but she would fight. He would regret this attack.

He continued. "I'm Nick. I assume you're aware of me since you've been following me since Seattle. At least that's what I'm assuming, or assumed until a few moments ago. I found you on Google and realized we may be here for the same reason. If I'm wrong, then we can fight it out here on this bus, OK? But for now, can you at least listen to me?"

She stared at him for several minutes. The pressure on her hand never wavered, and she in turn didn't relent. He had stamina; she could feel that.

Finally, she nodded. Yes. She would listen.

He began, "Let me tell you about a hypothetical situation that may have actually happened," and he started to tell his story.

He'd noticed the strange texture of some kind of rope-like crisscross pattern across her shoulder when he slipped his hand across her shoulder and wondered if she'd worn some kind of body armor or vest beneath her light jacket. Weird, he thought she'd made it through customs with a vest. What the hell? TSA has really dropped its guard, he thought as he detailed the past few months of his life. When he finished, he said, "Nõnkos Zia, I'm going to release your hand. Please don't stab me with whatever you're hiding under that jacket, OK? Please?"

She said nothing and waited for him to make the first move. He released her hand as he'd said, and immediately she shoved the pen up to his throat, pressing it against his carotid artery. Breathing rapidly, she glared at him and said nothing. Her eyes never wavered as she glared at him with hate-filled eyes.

He relaxed. If he was wrong, he was dead; she would kill him, and that was that. No point in wrestling around now. He'd made his move, made the decision, and now it was in her court. Trusting his gut had been a way of survival for too long to stop now; if he was wrong, he would pay dearly. The question remained, had he been wrong?

Finally she said, "Remove your arm from around my shoulder," her accent thick and heavy. It wasn't a request. He pictured a mental image of dark, heavy smoke rolling out of a house fire he had responded to many years ago and thought, *Yes, that's it, that's what her accent is like, smoke billowing from an invisible fire raging underneath and just out of sight, waiting to explode.*

Finally she withdrew the pen, and the calculated conversation carefully began.

About an hour later, he was still alive. She was calmer now but still had the pen under her jacket ready.

They were both quiet for a moment, saying nothing as they processed the information they'd shared. Finally, Nick spoke.

"Is it safe to say something about this is wrong, very wrong? I mean, the fact that this mission isn't State Department sanctioned, and yet Jay asked you to observe and report on the mission. Doesn't make sense, does it?"

"No, it does not."

"So why are you here?"

Nõn paused for a moment and then quietly said, "Because I have a personal connection to human trafficking. If I have the opportunity to do something about it, I am going to try; sitting back and doing nothing is not acceptable."

"Not acceptable? Seriously, you may die on this mission, is that acceptable?"

Nõn didn't answer; she'd faced death many times and always found a way to survive. She felt she was on borrowed time anyway; if her guardian hadn't interfered so many years ago, she would already be dead. She didn't fear death, neither did she seek danger. She just did what needed to be done.

"You must have some kind of death wish to be here today."

She replied, "No, no death wish; just a mandate, an agreement I made many years ago. A promise I must keep, that is all."

He rolled his eyes. "A mandate from who? God? A spirit guide? Jesus? Really? Did you sit in the woods and chant, eat mushrooms, beat on a drum, and wait for a spirit animal to show you the way?"

She didn't like the way this man spoke to her, or about her spirit guide. He was rude and condescending. She felt herself getting angry with his lack of respect for her beliefs. Then it hit her, why is that the assumption he came to? Takes one to know one? Perhaps.

She countered, "Why are you here, then, mister 'wild card'? Do you really think at your age you have anything meaningful to contribute to an operation like this? Seriously? What is your true motivation? What is your mandate? Honestly, do you buy this 'wild card' garbage?"

Nick looked hard at the driver of the bus and thought. To admit to her why he'd come was difficult. It sounded insane, but the more he thought about it, the more he had to admit he was here for one reason, and one reason only.

Finally, he replied, "I don't think you'll want to know why I'm here. I have no idea what your life experience is. I get hints from the biography I read online that your life hasn't been easy. You seem to be one of those people who believes in the system, in justice. If that's true, you won't understand my reason for being here."

Quietly, she replied, "It was not a question; it was a statement, an ultimatum." He would answer, or this conversation was over. Carefully, she spoke the words again, emphasizing each word. "Why are you here?"

His eyes glazed over, and he began to speak. "All of my adult life, I've tried to do what's right, right by the system. I was a part of the system, I worked within it. I'm tired of being bound by rules that don't fit the crime. I don't want justice anymore. I asked Jay if we'd be taking prisoners, bringing people to justice. He said there will be no prisoners. That's why I'm here."

She watched his face as he spoke and realized what he was saying and what he wasn't saying, possibly couldn't say.

"You are here seeking vengeance?" she said, realizing as she spoke the words what that statement implied.

He said nothing.

Overhead, the bus driver announced, "Folks, we'll be arriving in Moses Lake in five minutes. It would be a good time to prepare yourselves and gather your belongings. Please make sure to check around your seat and in the pockets and magazine holder in the chair in front of you to make sure you don't lose any items. Thank you for traveling with Greyhound."

He ignored her question and said, "Look, we have five minutes. In my world, it's best if everyone doesn't know what you know. What I mean by that is I think it's best if no one knows we've spoken, or for that matter even know each other. That way, we'll get a true read on what's going on, we can watch out for each other, perhaps pick up on something that's said or done that wouldn't have happened if they knew we'd talked. Make sense?"

She thought about the subtle admission there, carefully hidden in those words, and the idea as well that showing everything to everyone was rarely good. Finally, she nodded and said, "Yes. We will keep this between us." The statement answered all his questions.

"Good, I'll return to my seat. Good to meet you, Nõnkos Zia. I'm sure we'll speak again soon." And then as an afterthought, both joking and serious, he smiled and said, "Try not to stab me then, OK? Oh, and how the hell did you get through security with that vest on under your shirt? I thought the TSA was paying closer attention these days."

Nõn skillfully dodged the question and smiled. "Nick, you are not pronouncing my name correctly. It is pronounced 'Nyen', like the Japanese Yen, except the 'y' is soft."

Smiling, he said, "Cool, I like that, Nõn."

He returned to his seat and looked out the window at Moses Lake Washington. *Never thought I'd return to "Moses Hole"*, he thought to himself. *It's changed. More shops, streets, businesses, but still "the Hole" is still a hole.*

CHAPTER 10

Departing the bus, they were met by a shuttle/cab whose driver leaned against the 18-passenger Chevy van and held up a sign with two names written on it, Nõnkos Zia and Nick Hudson. They each walked up to the cab and introduced themselves; Nõn went first, and Nick followed a few moments later. They each loaded their own luggage into the van and got in, sitting several seats apart.

The driver asked the usual questions: "First time in Moses Lake? Traveling for business, or pleasure?"

Nõn was surprised when Nick admitted to being in Moses Lake many years ago, but she made sure she let nothing show. She listened while he detailed the story of the military deployment in the 80s and understood intuitively he was talking so she wouldn't have to. He was sharing his history more for her benefit than the driver's, while pretending to ignore her. She thought to herself, *Very tactical and careful, this one. I will need to pay special attention to what he does; seems every comment and movement have multiple meanings and layers.*

The trip was short. A few minutes later, they were unloading their luggage and walking inside the building where they would be staying until they left on the mission. Once inside, Nick went to the front desk first and began to check in. Talking to the clerk, he again started to communicate in layers.

"Wow, you guys sure have a lot of cameras here. Theft a problem? I mean, do I need to watch myself in this sleepy little town?"

She hadn't noticed the cameras, but now she was aware of them. They were everywhere, watching everything. Why?

The clerk said no, theft wasn't a problem, but they were a requirement for insurance purposes. Security systems kept the insurance rates down for the management.

Nick countered, "Insurance? Really? OK. Well, good to meet you, William. It is William, right? I mean, that's what your nametag says."

"Yes, sir. William."

"Call me Nick, William."

"Enjoy your stay, Nick," William said with a smile, but he wasn't smiling, not really.

Nick left the desk, and Nõn stepped up to the desk and proceeded to check in, now aware of the cameras and the passive-aggressive clerk.

Walking down the hallway on the main floor, Nõn was grateful to be staying in a room by herself. Not that she expected to be staying with anyone else; she just liked having the privacy of having the room to herself. Fewer questions that way. She began to unpack her clothes and connect her computer to the free wi-fi provided by the manager. Thinking for a moment, she stopped and disconnected the computer from the wi-fi system. Better to hotspot with her phone; Nick's observation of what was obvious, and yet not so obvious, was starting to change her mind set. Better to be safe than sorry. Once the computer was connected to the web, she typed in "Nick Hudson" in the search window and started to research her partner in crime.

Two hours later, she hadn't learned much. Nick had been married and divorced more times than most men. A few articles about shootings, court cases, and medals awarded. One very old article about some kind of military team. Seems Nick had a passion for fitness, or perhaps working out was a method to channel his obvious excess of energy. Something kept those marriages from working, either bad choices or the attraction to the wrong kind of people. Either way, both hinted at deeper conflicts.

She closed the laptop and was immediately startled by a double knock at the door. She got up quick and looked out the peephole. Nick was walking slowly down the hallway, dressed in running clothes. A quick knock to let her know he knew where she was and that he'd be going to scout out the area, under the ruse of going for a run. Amazing how quickly she understood his subtle messages, or did she?

Nick needed to get out, run, move, do something. Movement was survival in his world. That was a lesson he'd learned very early. Keep moving. Running was an easy outlet. He knocked on her door to let her know he was going out and would be back. Just in case. No idea if she'd understand what that knock meant, but best to C.Y.A. They were in this now, all in.

Jay was looking out the second story window as Nick went out for a run.

The clerk had called to let him know the last two members of the team had arrived. The clerk had no idea they were part of the team, only that the guy in room 215 had asked to be called when they arrived. Jay thanked the clerk and asked if he'd noticed anything unusual about their arrival. Anything at all?

The clerk thought about it and said, "No, just some weird chit chat with the guy, something about cameras, and theft in the building. The woman said nothing at all, but seemed polite."

Jay thanked him. Hanging up, he thought, *Once a cop, always a cop. Jesus, when does this guy ever shut down? One thousand miles from home, and this idiot is concerned about theft?*

A few miles later, Nick returned. The run felt good, a quick shower and maybe get something to eat, then sleep. Same basic routine he'd adhered to the last time he was at "the Hole." Walking down the hallway, he returned to the room. Opening the door, he saw an envelope on the floor; apparently, it had been slid under the door.

The phone rang.

"Nick, it's Jay. How was the run?"

"Good, how are you?"

"Good, just calling to let you know we'll meet for breakfast in the lobby in the morning and I'll answer any questions you have then. Is there anything you need now?"

"Nope, just gonna go get some food after a shower. Any recommendations on local restaurants?"

"Hmm, I've been told the Porterhouse Steakhouse is good. Pricey, but good."

"Thanks, I'll check it out."

"See you in the morning, then."

"What time again?"

"0730 hours. Sharp."

"Cool, see you then."

Opening the envelope, Nick wondered who it was from. The contents quickly made that clear. A note said, "Hotspot your Internet and e-mail me at this address. Nõn."

BREAKFAST

Through a series of e-mails, Nick and Nōn determined she'd been invited to lunch the next day, while he'd been invited to breakfast. Apparently, neither was supposed to be aware of the other, and Jay was making every effort to keep them separated as long as he could.

Nick and Jay met in the lobby the next morning at 0730. Nick arrived 30 minutes early to be sure he would miss nothing. However, there was nothing to miss; Jay arrived at 0730, right on time (late to the standard Nick lived by). They shook hands and walked out to the car Jay had rented for the remainder of the week. Jay made a point out of taking Nick on a tour of Moses Lake, detailing the local history, unaware Nick had been temporarily stationed in "The Hole" in the early 80s. Nick let him talk, noting that any knowledge he claimed to have had of "The Hole" was able to be obtained on a quick search of the Internet and Wikipedia. Jay needed to be in control, or at least feel in control of everything and everyone; it would be an easy trait to manipulate. Take away his control, and his ass would pucker so hard it would suck the fabric off the rental car's bucket seats.

They arrived about forty-five minutes later at Shari's Restaurant and Pies. Jay ordered coffee and a steak and eggs breakfast with toast, making sure the waitress understood he wanted the toast to be browned, not black, and the coffee to be extra hot. Also, he wanted the eggs over medium, not over easy, and the yolks could not be broken. Nick watched with amusement while the waitress took down the notes, barely concealing her annoyance.

Nick ordered decaf coffee and one hardboiled egg, and as an afterthought he asked for water, extra cold, and smiled at the waitress. An obvious poke at the anal retentive control freak that sat across the table from him.

The waitress laughed and replied, "One extra cold water, coming up." Jay was not amused but said nothing. Nick smiled, watching Jay's obvious discomfort with being made fun of and thought to himself this is a good place for him to be in, always ducking and bobbing verbal jabs, never comfortable.

Finally the food arrived, and Jay checked the order. He sent back the coffee because it wasn't hot enough and found the rest of the meal to be barely adequate. Jay was the kind of customer who rarely tipped. Being a prick to strangers was just who he was; he rarely had to work at it. It was a skill that came naturally, and he embraced it fully.

Nick had finished his egg and was sipping the decaf coffee when Jay finally started his breakfast after having sent one of the eggs back for being cooked too much. The waitress would be earning her minimum wage today. Silently, Nick wondered how many times Jay ended up eating food that contained spit, snot, or urine just because he was such an asshole to the wait staff. The idea made Nick smile and let out a little chuckle.

"What's so funny?"

"Nothing, just a thought that came into my head. So anyway, when do I meet the tactical team?"

Jay put down his fork and knife and started the peculiar room scanning and carefully measured cadence of speech Nick had observed in The Mashhouse on their first meeting.

"Ahh, well Nick, I hadn't planned on you meeting the tactical team until take-off. That was the intended point of you being uninitiated and having an outsider's point of view. Remember 'the wild card'? That's why you're here."

Nick watched the constantly scanning eyes and listened to the carefully managed rhetoric flowing out of Jay's mouth.

"Well, then we have a problem, because there's no way I'm going on a mission with a team I don't know, and who doesn't know me. We at the very least have a meet and greet, or you, my friend, can find yourself another wild card. Period, non-negotiable. Make it happen, or I'm on the next bus to Spokane. Besides, you said at the beginning of our talks about this mission that the team leader would have to approve me. Did something change?"

Jay said nothing, but his face suddenly went the color of a 2-day-old baby who was screaming its lungs out. Nick wondered, *Is he screaming inside right now, silently? Definitely! Yes, the two-day-old baby deep inside of Jay is in an ear-splitting fury.*

Finally, after several minutes Jay spoke. "I'll see what I can do. I cannot guarantee anything. The team is a tight knit group, they don't like untrained outsiders. And that's your role, to be an outsider. But since you're so insistent, I'll talk to them."

"Thanks, Jay, I appreciate it. So is there anyone else going on our little camping trip I need to know about?"

It was a test to see how much Jay was really hiding. If he mentioned Nõn, then Nick could reasonably believe there were no other hidden agendas. If he didn't, then it was abundantly clear Jay was a manipulative dick and not to be trusted.

Jay replied innocently, "Ahh, no, no one else on the mission. Just you and the tactical team, and one or two support staff, like myself."

Nick smiled, thinking, *You lying prick!* He replied, "OK, well, then I guess I'll only need to meet the tactical team, then."

Breakfast was finally over, and they drove in silence back to the billeting office. Jay's tight-lipped and barely controlled facial twitches maintained the beet red color the entire way back to the building. Nick pretended to be unaware of Jay's outrage at his lack of respect. Nick smiled as he looked out the window at the bleak surroundings of "The Hole". Perhaps just like a two-day-old baby, Jay just needed to take a huge dump and he'd feel better.

When they arrived at the building, Jay told Nick he would be in shortly while he called to make preparations for the meeting he'd requested. Nick nodded and walked on alone.

"Talk to you later, Jay."

"Yes, we'll talk later."

Walking in the building, Nick saw there was a continental breakfast buffet set up in the foyer and Nõn was seated there eating, alone. He looked at her briefly and continued on to his room. They would message later, and he would update her on the mental chess game of his breakfast discussion with Jay.

MEET AND GREET

Two hours later, there was a knock at Nick's door. Looking out the peephole, he saw it was Jay, his face still baby rage red. Nick giggled a moment and then gained control of himself and opened the door with a straight face.

"Hey man, what's up?"

"Come with me, we're going to meet the team."

Nick grabbed a jacket and walked silently behind Jay to the car.

Five minutes later, they arrived at a sheet metal building that had been an aircraft hangar; now it was abandoned and apparently housed the tactical team. Walking in, he overheard bits and pieces of a conversation echo through the massive hangar.

"I'm serious. On my last mission in the sandbox, we had a reporter who was embedded with our unit, that bitch couldn't suck your cock enough…"

"You can see she…she's a veteran of many gang…"

Then laughter from several voices. Jay called out in a commanding and authoritative voice as they entered the only interior office in the hangar.

"Attent huuuh." The team immediately snapped up to the military stiff standing posture of attention. The room was instantly silent.

"At ease," Jay announced with less enthusiasm. "Gentlemen, as I discussed with you earlier, this is your one and only face to face with the outside member of your team, Nick Hudson. Nick, this is the team you will be working with. Take whatever time you feel necessary to get acquainted."

Jay turned and left the group of seven men to their conversation.

The team leader introduced himself with a hard handshake that he held too long, glaring into Nick's eyes.

"Rooney, team leader, and this is my team, Fossum, Garcia, Green, Rohlk, and my second in command, Johnson."

The men looked at Nick with an unfriendly, challenging gaze, looking him up and down, some smirking.

Rooney asked, "May I ask what exactly are your qualifications to be on my team, Nick?"

Nick held Johnson's gaze; he appeared to be the least open to the idea of Nick being on the mission, based on his body language and attitude. *Might as well get this show on the road*, Nick thought as he walked slowly towards Johnson.

"Sure, you may ask," Nick replied but provided no details, walking directly up to Johnson, purposefully entering his space until the two men's noses nearly touched.

No one said a word as Nick and Johnson glared at each other. A minute passed, and no one moved, the tension in the air was unmistakable. The team was not used to this kind of disrespect. Finally, Nick felt he'd made his point and broke eye contact.

"My experience? Two tactical teams in the civilian world, entry teams on both. Expert marksman, and 30 years of urban warfare. I worked alone, Rooney, never with the security blanket of a team. Never had the luxury of a backup that could hold his own in a real firefight."

Rooney smiled and replied, "And when was this urban warfare? The year Seventeen Seventy-Six? You and General George Washington cross the Potomac River holding hands and rubbing each other's dicks?"

The team laughed heartily. Nick didn't reply.

Rooney said, "Look, Nick, I'm sure you, Jack Lalanne and Richard Simmons had a great time making workout tapes and licking each other's balls on the side. In your day, I'm sure you probably popped a nut or two in some waitress' ass and called that combat. But let's just be clear, we don't want you on this mission. I don't want you on this mission. I personally think you're a danger to my team, and if you do anything but stay the fuck out of me and my team's way, I'll kill you. We clear? I don't care about whose cock you sucked in a foxhole during the Tet offensive in sixty-eight. Stay the fuck out of our way, and you might get to go back home to your rocker and television remote and pretend you're still in the fight. Still relevant."

Nick said nothing, showing no emotion, no reaction to the threat. He and Rooney stared at each other and said nothing for several moments. Finally, Nick said, "It's been good to meet you G.I. Joe wannabe motherfuckers. Hope you can back up the 'death from above' bullshit with something more than talk." He turned quickly and walked away.

Multiple "Fuck yous" erupted from the group, and then "Ya, that's right, keep walking, old man, right back to your nursing home and your piss-soaked Depends."

Nick smiled. Mission accomplished, the setup was perfect. The gauntlet had been thrown down, the challenge accepted.

Walking meekly outside, he looked up at Jay. Raising his eyebrows, he said, "That didn't go as well as I'd hoped. Perhaps you were right, this was a bad idea."

Relieved, Jay said, "I tried to tell you, perhaps now maybe you'll accept I do know what I'm doing?"

"Ya, sorry man, thanks for humoring me."

Jay returned them to the billeting office, and they went their separate ways.

CHAPTER 11

Once he was back in his room and the door was locked, he checked to make sure no one had been inside.

He'd set up his smartphone on record mode when he'd left, the smartphone's rear facing camera pointed at the doorway.

Checking the phone, he saw that no one had entered the room. Deleting the video files, he checked his e-mail. There was one message from Nõn.

"Nick, I had an interesting lunch with Jay, he was very quiet and obviously angry about something. Food was terrible, and the man is an absolute tyrant to the wait staff. Who knew anyone could be so picky about the temperature of his coffee? Regardless, I met the team we'll be working with in an abandoned hangar. They are what I expected, but not what I had hoped for. This is only about money for them. Money only! One of them mentioned that he would be willing to accept a blow-job for his personal protection during the mission. The others laughed. I guess there is something called a 'desert princess'? I explained I was not interested in his genitalia and that the only reason I was here was to document their mission. Not to be the team's sexual playmate. Some-one mentioned the term 'Camp meat?' Not sure what that means exact-ly, but in the context it was said, I assume it is sexual in nature. Anyway, I am not impressed by this 'team' we are going with. The only difference between them and the people they are going to hunt is who pays them. Just my opinion. Jay will be taking me into the town later. I need to go to the post office to pick up a package I mailed to myself before I left. Jay is picking me up at 2:30. Nõn."

Nick replied, "I met the team as well, laid the groundwork for a long and meaningful relationship. Could you pick me up a deck of cards, standard deck for poker would be great, and a suitcase of beer (a suitcase is a large cardboard container, usually 24 cans total). I prefer MGD brand if you can get it. If not, any beer will do. Thanks, Nick."

Jay arrived at Nõn's door at 1430 hours and knocked lightly on the door. She answered almost immediately, and he led her to a nearby door. She noticed they left the building walking out the door opposite the direction of Nick's room. Jay was very subtle in his efforts to keep them apart and unaware of each other. If she hadn't run into Nick in the airport and then spoken to him on the bus, she had to admit she would still be completely unaware of him.

At the post office, Nõn asked the clerk to check for a package that had been sent to her name in care of "general delivery." When she'd retrieved it, she felt relieved. She returned to the car and asked Jay if he would mind taking her to the store. She explained that she "wanted to pick up some supplies, she liked to drink a beer now and then and play solitaire at night. They both helped her sleep."

Jay said, "Sure, I get that. I like a drink now and then before bed. Not so much into solitaire, though." Nõn smiled.

Back at her room, Nõn wrote another email to Nick:

"Nick, I am back from the post office and store. I bought two decks of cards and two cases of beer, just in case someone wants to see either. Where would you like me to put your beer and cards so that you can get to them? Nõn."

A few moments later, Nick replied:

"Nõn, thanks much! Can you leave the beer and the cards behind the dumpster at the rear of the building? Just take them out in a sack after dark, like you were going to dump your garbage. I'll pick them up. Did you get your package from the post office? Oh, and can you put the beer in your fridge so it's cold? Nick."

Nõn wrote, "Nick, yes, I am relieved to have the package. I did not want to go on this trip without it, and it was a bit of stress trying to figure out how to get it here without a lot of problems. But it is here now, and I feel much better. Your beer is in the fridge. I will leave it where you asked. Is there anything new I need to be aware of?"

"Nõn, not yet. I'll keep in touch, don't wait up for me! Time to do some night ops. Wish me luck. BTW, use the front door to take your garbage out so you're on camera. Thanks again. Nick."

Nõn read the last message and deleted it. She hadn't seen anyone suspicious in the hotel yet, but she didn't want to leave anything to chance. She was remarkably relieved when she opened her self-addressed package and once again held her knife. Its crude shape and design were a comfort to her, as well as its considerable weight. She smiled as she checked the edge to make sure it was still razor sharp. Pulling up her sleeve, she ran the knife across her arm, barely letting the edge have contact with her skin. The tiny hairs on her forearm were immediately collected in a small clump. Her eyes glimmered; her talisman was back where it belonged, comfortably in her hand. She'd felt naked without it. Looking outside, she saw it was already dark. She hurried, gathering the beer and deck of cards in a bag for Nick and then left her room, walking down the hallway. She could hear the sound of the television; apparently, Nick was watching some game shows. She rolled her eyes; she hated game shows, mind-numbing garbage. Game shows weren't what she expected someone like Nick to spend his time watching.

Shrugging, she thought, *I guess you can never really tell what people are really about.*

Walking out of the lobby, Nõn made sure to make eye contact with the clerk and then walked out to the dumpster. As she walked behind it, she was barely aware of a shape moving in the dark. Immediately and instinctively, she dropped the sack and retrieved her knife from under her clothing. She quickly took up a stance any martial arts practitioner would describe as a "horse stance" and waited for the attack to begin.

No attack came. She called out to the shape quietly, "Come forward one step, and it will be your last." She heard a slight laugh, and then a reply.

Snickering, Nick said, "No, I'll stay where I am. I think I took enough risk letting go of your hand on the bus, Nõn. I don't want to be impaled on that bastardized Bowie knife you're carrying."

"Nick?"

"Yes, it's me," he said, then stepped out of the darkness. Dressed in black from head to toe, he'd completely blended in to the night shadows. She noticed he was incredibly quiet.

Stepping forward, he took the bag and said, "Thank you, I see your package was well stocked." He smiled as he motioned to the knife. "Glad to see you've graduated from ballpoint pens to something more substantial." He drifted back into the shadows.

She said, "I had this knife made for me many years ago. How did you get out of your room without me hearing the door close?"

From the darkness he said, "We're on the main floor, remember? I left my television on the timer setting and crawled out the window. I never opened or closed the door; that's why you heard nothing."

"So where are you going? What is going on? Why did you need the beer and deck of cards?"

Silence; not a sound from Nick.

"Nick?" A few seconds later, "Are you there?"

He was gone; just like that, he'd disappeared into the shadows. Not a sound, nothing to give away that he'd left. Nōn shuddered; the man was a mystery. No one moved that quietly. He did have some surprises. She was very uncomfortable now; he could be anywhere, and she didn't like the idea that he was watching her. She left quickly and walked back into the building. Walking past his room, she heard a man's voice yell out, "Come on down, you're the next contestant," and then a crowd erupted in applause. She smiled. *Always with the surprises, this one.*

Nick left quietly, making his way from shadow to shadow, making sure not to silhouette himself with any back lighting. He had to make his way onto the runway and then to the abandoned hangar without a mistake. If he was caught, then he would have some explaining to do, and the worst of it would be how he was able to get the beer and deck of cards. Their alliance would be discovered.

Forty minutes later, he was standing outside the hangar, listening. There was very little sound from inside the hangar. He had to wait for the right moment, or they'd be on him. There was little doubt of that outcome, his ass would be kicked most severely. Finally, he heard a collection of voices coming toward the door. He slipped into the shadows and disappeared. The metal door opened loudly, and four of the team members stepped outside into the darkness, and one lit up a cigarette and began to smoke. Nick slipped into the now open door quietly and unnoticed. He silently made his way to the office at the back of the hangar as the men outside began to talk among themselves. The other two were in here in the shadows somewhere. Finally, his eyes adapted to the complete darkness of the interior of the hangar. He could see some light from the outside and could now see the four men milling around in front of the door. Hugging the interior wall of the hangar, he took the long way to the office. Finally, he found the other two men. They were in the only other room in the hangar, a crude restroom and shower.

The only creature comfort the team had been allowed. This was perfect. Nick slipped into the office and set the cold suitcase of beer on the table. Quietly, he opened the package and set 6 beers on the table. Then he sat down and waited. Opening the deck of cards, he removed them and began to practice his shuffle.

The men finished their break and began to walk back into the hangar, talking among themselves and joking.

One voice piped up, "So what do you think that reporter is wearing now?"

"My guess is nothing, nothing at all," another voice said.

"Jesus, I would love to tap that ass! Did you see it? She has an ass like a twelve-year-old boy."

"Dude, only you would think a twelve-year-old boy had a hot ass."

They all broke out in laughter.

Then suddenly, "Quiet, quiet, do you hear that? What the hell is that?" someone whispered.

Nick kept shuffling and said, "Jack Lalanne and Richard Simmons wanted to be here tonight, but they were too busy having walker races at the old folks home. They send their best. Any one of you up for a beer and a friendly wager on a deck of cards?"

The group stepped into the light of the office and glared at Nick as he sat at the table, surrounded by beer. They formed a semi-circle around him as he sat, shuffling.

He smiled and said, "Gentlemen, I noticed an amazing lack of alcohol on my last visit. Step up and grab a beer, or if you prefer we can fight. Personally, I'd prefer a beer. It was a long walk to get here."

One of the men said, "Go get Rooney, now."

Another disappeared into the darkness, and a few moments later Rooney returned with the remainder of the team.

"Nick, I see you've returned. Still aching for an ass kicking, I see."

"No, not really. I just thought you John Rambo types might like a beer and a friendly wager with a Depends-wearing old man bearing gifts."

"What's the wager?"

"We each put a hundred dollars on the table and shuffle the cards. First time through the deck, each card is face value. Royalty are ten, aces are fifteen. Clear?"

BAROOTA: THE HUNTING GROUND

"Sure."

"Next time through, it doubles, then triples, and so on."

"What's the game?"

"Pushups. I pull a card, and we each do the number of pushups that's the number on the card. Last one doing pushups wins the pot. At first we all do the pushups together, and then rest 30 seconds after each card. Once it's down to only two players, they take turns. They only rest while the other guy is doing pushups. It's a contest me, Jack, and Richard came up with in the rest home. You guys up for it? Seven hundred bucks to the winner, and meanwhile you get about 4 beers each, on this old man's tab."

Nick reached into his pocket and pulled out a one hundred dollar bill. He slapped it down on the table. "Ante up, gentlemen."

Rooney said, "This won't take long, old man. We'll have your money and beer and send you on your way with a beat down you won't forget for some time."

Four hours later, there were two people left doing pushups, Rooney and Nick.

"So explain to me how the hell you got into the hangar and no one noticed?"

"I taught Johnny English everything he knows."

The group laughed, and Rooney said, "No, serious, man, how did you get in?"

"I used a trick I learned the night of the Tet offensive. Can't share it with you, sorry. National secrets, you understand."

The two men were exhausted and stalling for time. Garcia drew an ace, and Nick went first. The group counted while he painfully forced out seventy-five pushups.

Rooney was next. Garcia drew a card, seven. Rooney did thirty-five pushups.

Garcia drew another card, a king.

Nick finished fifty pushups, sweat dripping off his face onto the concrete floor.

Garcia drew another card, a ten of clubs.

Rooney punched Garcia in the chest and dropped to do fifty more pushups. Garcia laughed as he barely made the last rep. Garcia drew another card, another ace.

Nick dropped down to do his seventy-five pushups, and the room went quiet. At 60, he stopped and said, "Wait a goddamn minute, that was the fifth ace in this shuffle. I made sure there were only four aces when we started. You assholes stacked the deck!"

The room erupted in laughter. Garcia and Green were rolling on the floor. Rooney, laughing so hard he could barely speak, said, "Ya, we stacked the deck. We started stacking the deck when it came down to just me and you. Jesus, you, Jack and Richard must do some serious shit in that fucking rest home, old man! The pot is yours. Take it. I was out fifteen cards ago. Have a beer, old man, there's one left."

An hour later, Nick was crawling back through the window of his room. He was sore, covered in sweat, but had achieved his goal. The ice between them was broken. The team was nothing but mercenaries, just like Nõn had said. There would be no loyalty from them or between them. They were here for the money and the money only, but at least now they understood he had a skill set to bring to this mission that was worthwhile. More than the pushups, sneaking in unnoticed and setting up the beer and cards like he did had an impact on their perception of him. No one had figured that one out; best they didn't know how simple it really was. Really, better to keep them guessing, he thought as he slid into bed, exhausted.

CHAPTER 12

Running through the hallway, Nick was trying to find a child he could hear screaming. The air was filled with smoke, making it hard to see and breathe. Smoke was everywhere and thick. Disoriented, he dropped to his knees; the air was better down here, and he could at least see the hallway in front of him. Crawling as fast as he could, he knew this was going south fast. He had to find the child and get both of their asses out of the building before the floor beneath them collapsed into the fire raging one floor below. The child's screams were horrifying and shrill, pain-filled screams of agony that ended only when its lungs were void of air. The pattern repeated, screams, silence, then more screaming. Everything slowed down, and his legs became heavy, too heavy. He was losing strength, losing the will to go on, more screams. Finally, the flames burst through the floor and he was engulfed in fire. He panicked and screamed. The pain was indescribable. He'd been told you pass out when you're engulfed in a fire and you'd never feel a thing, you just died. It wasn't true; his body was on fire, and he felt everything. The skin crackled and peeled back, charred his eyelids, pulled back, leaving the balls of gelatin exposed. He felt them erupt, and liquid flowed down his cheeks. He inhaled to scream, and his lungs were filled with fire. He tried to scream, but all that came from his lungs were smoke and fire. As he was spitting fire from his own lungs, the child screamed again. Nothing he could do now, he was dying. The child screamed again.

Nick shot up in bed, soaked with sweat. The child's scream morphed into the phone ringing. Breathing hard, his lungs hurt, his throat felt burned and strained, as if he actually had been screaming in terror. His chest, arms, and back were all aching and stiff. Reaching for the phone, his arms and back were quick to remind him of the stupidity of the previous night's events. Finally, fumbling, he reached the phone, still shaking from the memory of the dream. His hands and feet tingled painfully, and his eyes had a hard time focusing.

Jesus, I feel old, he thought as he picked up the phone.

"Ya? What?"

It was Jay. "Ya? Is that how you answer the phone, really? Ya? Jesus, where were you? I let the phone ring maybe ten times."

"Sorry, man, I was in the shower. What's up?"

"What's up is we have a mission briefing today in a half-hour. Think you can make that, or do you need to get back to that shower?"

"Ya, I'll be there. Meet in the lobby? When?"

"Meet in the lobby in half an hour. Don't be late." Jay hung up.

A quick five-minute, sore muscled, pain-filled shower later, Nick was getting dressed and walking out the door. There was no one in the hallway. He was grateful for that; it gave him time to stretch and loosen up a little. Jesus, he was sore. Working the soreness out of his arms, back and chest would take some time.

Entering the lobby, he saw they were just setting up for the continental breakfast. He looked for a clock; seeing none, he asked the clerk setting up the coffee and Danish, "What time is breakfast?"

The clerk replied, "Breakfast is served every day beginning at seven a.m., until eight thirty a.m."

Damn, it was nearly seven a.m. He'd only been asleep four hours, just long enough for the soreness to set in and the nightmares to set up shop and torment him once again.

Sitting down, he waited for the clerk to finish setting up the coffee pots and pastry cart. Getting up to pour himself a cup of decaf, he heard the door open behind him.

It was Nõn. She ignored him and walked up to the coffee and pastries and quietly whispered, "Did you hear all that screaming this morning? It sounded like someone was being killed, and then it just stopped."

"Screaming? Nope, didn't hear a thing."

"It was horrible. To be honest, I thought it sounded like you."

He shook his head no but wouldn't make eye contact with her as he sipped his coffee and turned around to go back to his chair. She watched him carefully and noticed the stiffness in his gait, and how carefully he sat down in the chair.

I wonder what happened last night? she thought.

She sat down at another table and began to read a paper she'd picked up at the front desk. They ignored each other until Jay arrived.

Jay entered the room from the hallway and said, "Good to see you both, glad you're here early so we can do the introductions." He said, "Nick, this is Nõn. She'll be joining us today. Nõn, this is Nick. He's a pain in the ass, and he too is on the team."

Nick smiled, Jay did not. Nõn and Nick shook hands and pretended they hadn't met.

"So what do you do, Nõn?"

"I am a freelance journalist. Mostly I do humanitarian pieces to raise the public's awareness of people who are being victimized."

"Interesting. Good fit, I would guess, for this little trip."

"And you, Nick? What do you do?"

"Recently, I mostly piss off Jay, apparently. Before that, I was a cop, pretty much all I've ever done."

"And what does a cop have to contribute to a mission like this?" asked Nõn.

"Comic relief, that's what all cops do, comedy. Haven't you ever watched Reno 911? Police Academy?"

Nõn rolled her eyes, playing her part expertly. She said, "Fine, funny man. Don't answer my question. I would guess you barely graduated high school as well. Keep this in mind while you amuse only yourself. I take my job seriously, so keep your funny man jokes to yourself."

"No can do, missy, the jokes flow from me like water from a lake. You're just gonna have to deal with it."

Jay interrupted, "I can see you two are off to a great start. Seems you have the same effect on everyone you meet, Nick," the hostility rolling off him in waves as he glared at Nick.

Nick shrugged his shoulders. "Heard it my whole life, Jay. I'm a world class asshole. Nothing new there."

Jay and Nõn both rolled their eyes, and Jay said, "OK, well enough chitchat, let's get on the road."

Walking to the car, Nõn opened the front passenger door and got in, sitting next to Jay. Nick got in the back seat.

"This reminds me of the scene from 'As Good As it Gets'. Ever watch that one, Jay? Jack Nicholson goes on a road trip with his gay neighbor and the hot waitress that serves him breakfast. Here we are just finishing breakfast. Nõn could be considered sort of hot, I guess. And here we are sitting in the car. Me being, well…me in the back seat and older. Guess that makes you the gay neighbor, huh Jay?"

Jay said nothing, but his face returned to the bright baby rage red it had the previous day. Nõn said nothing as well and looked out her window, shaking her head.

"OK, then, shall we?" Nick smiled, looking in the rearview mirror, matching Jay's furious glare as he raised and lowered his eyebrows rapidly.

The mission briefing was held in a typical drab unremarkable building, left over from some previous government deployment. The building was typical of government construction. Poorly heated, bad plumbing, and flooring made of industrial grade floor tiles that had long since had any pattern or texture buffed out of them. Anyone in government service will tell you there is a nearly insane compulsion by the higher ups to have their floors shine like they were brand new. So the industrial grade tiles in every building that received any use at all are buffed until the original designs are completely removed. For Nick, this was old home week. This building housed Moses Hole's Central Security Control, or C.S.C. The room the briefing would be held in was what had been the Guardmount room, the daily briefing room for security forces before they were taken to post. Nick whistled the theme song to "Welcome Back Kotter" as they walked through the hallways. No one appreciated his humor, or how ironic this whole goddamn mission was turning out to be.

Jay said, "What's that you're whistling, Nick? It sounds familiar."

"Was I whistling? Hmm, I wasn't aware of it, sorry."

Jay, more frustrated, thought, *I can't wait to wipe that smile off your face, funny man. Your time is coming.*

Nick and Nõn sat down; Nõn in the front row like a good student would, and Nick all the way in the back, as far from the front as he could be. In school, it drove his teachers insane to have students take the back row when there were plenty of seats up front. Teachers, however, didn't live in his world. In that world, being able to see everyone in the room at the same time could mean the difference between survival and, well, not surviving. It was an observation point, tactical in nature. Teachers had no understanding of tactics or survival. Teachers loved the students in the front row.

A few minutes later, the room filled up with the tactical team, Jay, and the flight crew. Jay closed the door and immediately puffed up like a lion fish. His chest swollen with authority and his voice now boomed, filling the room.

"Quiet down, everyone, quiet down."

Nick rolled his eyes as he noticed the room had been quiet, no one had been speaking. This speech had been well rehearsed and apparently made Jay feel like he was in more control.

"OK, we all know why we're here. I'm going to go around the room and have each of you introduce yourselves, starting with the flight crew."

Nick listened while the squeaky clean flight crew introduced themselves. James Muir was the pilot, John Allen the co-pilot, and the navigator's name was Mike Hunt. The tactical team erupted in a wave of snickers and laughter at that disclosure.

Nick got the joke, who the hell named their child Mike Hunt? It was one of those names used in juvenile phone pranks. You called a business and asked them to page Mike Hunt, it was an emergency. If it worked and they actually paged that name, it sounded like "My Cunt" over the loudspeakers. "Paging My Cunt." Nick had to admit, he'd pulled that one a few times as a kid, and honestly once at a staff meeting as a cop on the Chief of Police. That prank nearly got him fired from the department. The Chief had no sense of humor, who knew?

Anyway, the tactical team was next, and they were introduced by Rooney, the team leader. Nick watched from the back of the room as Rooney detailed each team member's name and role on the team. Apparently, Fossum was their demolitions expert. Interesting. Every tactical team had one. The one crazy guy who liked to blow shit up.

Next came Nõn's turn. She stood up and introduced herself. Green and Johnson started to make moaning noises, and Garcia pushed his tongue against his cheek, simulating a blow job while she spoke.

Nick thought, *Once we leave U.S. air space, this is going to be a problem. These fuckheads really are gonna try to get her alone; hopefully, she doesn't kill them before the mission is complete.*

He made a mental note to keep close to her. She could handle herself, without a doubt, but six against one were odds that could only be beaten in the movies.

Nõn ignored the tactical team and sat down.

Next, Jay asked Nick to introduce himself.

Nick stood up. "Hi, I'm Nick Hudson. I've met most of you before this meeting. The tactical team and I hit it off well, and Nõn and I are besties. My role, as Jay has put it, is to act as a 'Wild Card', an unexpected element to fill in the gaps should the tactical 'Zero Dark Thirty' crew (raising his voice) FUCK THINGS UP! I'll try to do my best."

He formed the familiar hand position universally recognized as "the bird" or "Fuck you" and made a mock casual salute towards Rooney and his team. Rooney, glaring at Nick, returned the gesture, emphasizing it with a quick, angry snap of a salute. Nick smiled and sat down.

Jay said, "Yes, well now that we all know who we are, let's get started on the mission briefing. James Muir, you have the floor."

Muir stood up and began his briefing. Apparently, the plan was to stay within established flight corridors within the U.S. Muir explained flight corridors were like roads for aircraft. Once they left the United States, they'd be traveling well known flight paths that were used for illegal drug trafficking. The paths were well documented and commonly used. The plan would be to go dark, meaning no radio traffic unless necessary. The plane would fly out over the Pacific Ocean and then return to land once they approached the Darien Gap. Muir explained they'd be landing at the Sambu Airfield located in the Darien Gap. That concluded his part of the mission, and the mission briefing.

Jay stood up. "Yes, when we arrive at the Darien Gap, we'll disembark the plane with our equipment. We'll be traveling over land on rough roads to the base camp. The base camp is code named 'Baroota'. It means 'The Hunting Ground'.

Once we're there, Team Leader Rooney will begin final planning for the extraction of 12-15 persons of interest. These 'persons of interest' are the reason we're all here. Make no mistake, people, this will not be an easy extraction. Our objective is heavily guarded and protected by trained and armed personnel. It will be a fight, gentlemen, and lady. But we have the advantage of surprise and night vision equipment. We'll overcome their force and return safely. I want this mission to go by the numbers, with no screw-ups. Any questions?"

The tactical team erupted in a well-timed and obviously practiced, "WHo-Rah."

No one said a word.

Jay continued, "Good, we leave tonight at 2100 hours. I'll be picking up Nick and Nõn, the rest of you will meet at the time and location we've already discussed. Dismissed."

Nick got up and left the room, walking out ahead of the rest. This "WHo-Rah" shit got on his nerves. Nothing ever went like it was planned.

You can beat your chest all damn day, he thought. *Doesn't mean dick when the shit hits the fan. Nothing ever went by the numbers.*

Already, the mindset was wrong. Flexible and fluid was the only way to survive in tactical situations. Only an admin prick like Jay spewed this Hollywood, "by the numbers" bullshit. Barely able to hide his disgust, a now surly Nick waited at the car for Nõn and Jay.

Back in the room, Nick sat and waited for an e-mail from Nõn. It took several minutes for her e-mail to finally show up on the smartphone.

"Nick, informative meeting, yes? I am going to the post office to send my computer back to my home. No point in bringing it along to such a remote area. I did some research on the Darien Gap. It is one of the most remote areas in the world and is nearly void of any real roadways. So it will be an interesting trip, no doubt. Hopefully, you and Rooney won't kill each other while you are out rescuing the kidnapped victims. Do you really think it is wise to be so confrontational with them? Not my business, but you will be out in the jungle with them, alone. Jay has told me that I will not be included on any extraction operations. They don't want to risk it. I explained that I have been in dangerous places before, but he would not budge.

I looked up Baroota, the name of the compound. It is an aboriginal word, and it does indeed mean the hunting ground. Interestingly, I found another word similar to it during my search, 'Nokunno'. It is also an aboriginal word as well and is used as the name of a mythical being who went about by night killing people. The name describes an imaginary being, like a man, who prowls at night and kills, an assassin. After your disappearing stunt last night, melting into the shadows like you did, leaving me there talking to no one but myself, I thought it fitting. That is my nickname for you now, Nick-Nokunno the Assassin."

Nick replied, "Nõn, Rooney and I have no disagreement, no worries, just a friendly testosterone contest. Nothing to worry about. Besides, I've never played well with the other kids in the playground, why try to change now? Nokunno, huh? I like it. At least you didn't name me 'Fred' or something ridiculous. I'm going to get some sleep, and I would advise you to do the same after mailing your laptop. Things are likely to get very intense very soon, and sleep won't be easy to come by. See you at the plane. Nick."

CHAPTER 13

Nick woke up at 6 pm to the sound of his smart phone buzzing. He'd received a text. Unlocking the phone, he saw that JoAnn had finally responded. The message said, "Good luck on your hunting trip, see you in two weeks. Knock them dead, Love J."

He responded, "Sorry for how this has turned out. I'll be back in one week, babe. I hope to make it up to you then. Thanks, and take care. Nick."

She never listened. He told her it would be one week, over and over while they argued. It would only be one week. She was especially mad when he wouldn't accompany her on the last trip she'd made to North Carolina. It was the week Jay had called to tell him the mission was a go. He knew time was getting short and tried to explain that to her, but she wouldn't listen. After Jay had called, he was glad he'd refused to go. Every day he could train was critical. She'd barely spoken to him after that trip. There was a rift between them that was unbridgeable. He was glad to see the text message; maybe there was still hope for them after this mission was complete. He was hopeful.

Nick waited for a response to the text he'd sent. It never came. Nick fell back asleep, hopeful and also grateful for the sleep sans nightmares.

At 8 pm Nick woke, rested and showered again. *Probably the last shower this week*, he thought. Not much chance of running hot water in the jungle. Dressing in his Black 5-11 tactical gear, he looked in the mirror. Startled, he expected a younger face to be staring back at him; instead of the man he felt he still was, there was an angry grey haired old man looking back at him. Muscled, yes, fit as well, but wrinkled, old and grey. Funny how he felt twenty-five mentally and physically until he looked into the mirror.

"Fuck you," Nick said angrily at the ridiculous image in the mirror. "Fuck you, motherfucker."

Nick turned off the light and left the room.

Jay arrived a few minutes after Nick in the foyer of the building. Nõn was already waiting for both of them, dressed in her usual long-sleeved baggy shirt and denim pants. They walked quietly to the car and drove to the waiting plane, warming up on the tarmac. Nick recognized the aircraft as a C-130.

He took a deep breath, thinking, *Well, this is going to be a bumpy and noisy ride.*

Jay handed them both earplugs and told them to put them in now as he escorted them to the passenger door of the aircraft. The cargo door was also open, and aircraft parts were being loaded onto the back of the plane. The tactical team's gear was already loaded, as were the six tactical team members. Everyone was ready to go. The loadmaster secured the equipment to the cargo tie down points and then walked to the front of the plane to let the flight crew know they were all set. Nick saw they would be sitting in jump seats, cloth straps sewn together in a mesh pattern.

Asshole Jay spared no expense this trip, he thought. Jump seats were going to be really uncomfortable but weighed almost nothing.

Jay took a seat next to Nõn, while Nick sat near the others on the opposite side of the plane. The loadmaster, still wearing headphones and safety glasses, went alone at the edge of the row of jump seats and lay down across the empty seats to sleep. Verbal communication wasn't possible. The plane was loud, even with the ear protection. If they needed to communicate, he and Nõn would have to do it carefully.

Five minutes later, Nõn felt the vibrations of the engines of the aircraft increase and the plane began to move. Taxiing down the runaway, the vibrations of the cracks and spacers in the concrete runway came vibrating through the aircraft frame, slowly first, then increasing rapidly as the plane accelerated, and then they were off.

The vibration and noise of the aircraft were mind-numbing, and eventually Nick too fell asleep. It seemed wise; sleep would be a rare commodity soon.

An unknown amount of hours later, they landed; apparently the plane needed to refuel. The trip would be nearly five thousand miles as the crow flies, longer since they had to take the surreptitious route that had been chosen. They would refuel twice during the trip, where? Nick had no idea. It had never been discussed at the briefing. While they refueled, the passengers took turns in the rudimentary restroom facilities on the plane. No one was allowed to leave the plane under any circumstances.

At the eight-hour mark, the loadmaster came to each of them with an opened MRE and a bottle of water. Nick nodded, taking the food and water, and mouthed, "Thank you" as the loadmaster moved on to the next person. The loadmaster handed Rooney a large plastic bag and motioned to throw the garbage in after the meal was completed. The loadmaster then motioned a thumbs up. Rooney returned the thumbs up in acknowledgement; he understood. Once everyone was fed, the loadmaster returned to the jump seats and ate as well. The garbage bag went from person to person until all the used meals were inside of it. Occasionally, Nick would look at Nõn. She never made eye contact with him; she was either sleeping or reading the entire trip.

Eighteen hours into the flight, the loadmaster got up and began to hand out a third bottle of water to the occupants of the plane. The same garbage bag routine was done, and then the loadmaster went to the flight cabin and gave them water as well. Greeted with smiles and waves, the crew gratefully accepted the water.

Standing at the front of the plane, the loadmaster watched as the tactical team, Nõn and Nick all finished their water. Nick knew it had been a long flight; his legs and back ached from sitting in the jump seats for so long, so it wasn't surprising when the loadmaster started to stretch and do some exercises to limber up. Nick was getting sleepy and decided to close his eyes for a moment. Odd, he thought as he started to drift off to sleep. He didn't see the loadmaster give Jay a bottle of water. Nick thought the loadmaster probably didn't like the prick either. Smiling, Nick fell deeply asleep.

Wind rushed through the aircraft, and for a moment Nick was aware of the feeling of extreme cold and noise. It felt like being in a hurricane; he couldn't remember where he had been or how he got to where he was. The floor he was lying on felt like metal and was very cold, his head repeatedly bouncing off the surface. He felt no pain, just the impact of his cheek bouncing off the metal flooring.

Where am I now? Where have I been?

He couldn't remember.

Finally, the wind died down and the noise lessened. He felt a warm rain sprinkling down on his face and turned to face the rain. It felt better than the cold floor. Then the darkness of sleep closed in around him.

CHAPTER 14

At the exact moment Nick was giving Rooney the middle finger salute in the mission briefing, Pat had just arrived at Moses Lake. She checked into billeting and immediately went to her room to sleep. It had been a long flight from the east coast, with many layovers and plane changes. She was tired and had much to prepare for. Setting the alarm on her smartphone, she lay down and immediately was asleep. She slept until 4 pm and then woke up and turned off the alarm, showered and got dressed, and then went over the game plan Jay had set up.

She was to act as the loadmaster for the flight, making sure the spare parts were well secured, the food and water were taken care of for the long flight. No one was to see her face or have any conversations with her. Once they were over the ocean and at the designated point, she would distribute the final bottle of water. That's when things would get interesting.

Long ago when she'd taken an exam for her job with the Forest Service, she'd been told she'd failed. Her test results had been described as "concerning" by the HR representative. What the hell that meant, she had no idea; it was clear, however, "concerning" meant she wasn't going to be able to fly for the Forest Service. What it did mean was she'd scored off the charts in an area called the dark triad. That was a disqualifier. She was out.

A couple of days later, a man had come to her apartment door and introduced himself. He said he was there to see if she was still interested in the job with the Forest Service as a pilot.

"Hell yes, I am, but I bombed the psych exam," was her reply.

"What if I can get that aspect of the process to be overlooked? Would you be interested?"

"Sure, what's the catch? You aren't doing this because it's 'do a good deed day' in Washington."

"The catch is you would also be working for us on the side, flying missions that are, shall we say, off the books. Not exactly the kind of missions we want publicized in the media, or brought to the attention of Congress."

"So that whole bullshit about concerning test results is gonna be swept under the rug?"

"The 'concerning test results' like yours are exactly what we're looking for, so are you in or not?"

"Yes, but who will I be really working for? The N.S.A, the C.I.A, the F.B.I?"

"You'll be working for the Forest Service. When I call, you'll do what we ask, and then go back to work for the Forest Service. The rest is above your pay grade, understood?"

She understood.

And so she began a long and successful career with the Forest Service, until three years ago. The whole bruised peach program (her pet name for it) was scrapped, and suddenly she was out, no longer valued, no more secret missions, and she was banned from flying and posted to a desk, shuffling papers and answering the phone. There was no explanation as to why or what happened, and she didn't dare ask. She'd seen too much by that point to know better than to ask questions. You didn't ask; if you did, you would disappear. Literally.

That was then; now she was back in six-figure land, making the real money again. The call had come in, and she'd answered. She had a skill set that was valued in some dark circles, and apparently someone in one of those circles had mentioned her name. She was able to do what others wouldn't, and she did it well.

At 1800, she was on the tarmac loading the aircraft. The squeaky clean flight crew approached the aircraft and waved to her before they entered the aircraft and started their preflight checklists. She watched, amused, thinking to herself, *I bet these candy asses passed the psych exam, too bad they had no idea a graduate of the "Dark Triad Program" would be on board, carefully disguised as a lowly loadmaster.*

The tactical crew arrived and loaded their equipment and ignored her. She watched as they loaded several large metal containers and then motioned to them she would secure them. They nodded and sat down, strapping into the jump seats. Too bad, really, she thought as she watched. She should have arrived a few days earlier and spent some quality time with a couple of them. They looked like they understood exactly what a woman like her was looking for in a party. That idea made her smile. Oh well, another time perhaps.

The rest of the team finally arrived, and she watched as Jay escorted a redheaded black woman and an older grey haired guy to the plane. The old guy walked like he was stiff, probably arthritis, she thought. The black girl looked familiar, but she couldn't remember from where.

The plane finally took off. She went to the end of the row of jump seats and lay down. This was familiar territory for her.

After feeding the team and distributing water, she'd remained awake, waiting for the signal from Jay. At last, he nodded to her that it was time. She got up and went to a separate package of water bottles and began to hand them out to the teams. Then she went into the cockpit and gave the flight crew each a bottle. They were sheep; smiling, they accepted the bottles and gratefully drank the tainted contents. She went to the cargo area and began stretching, watching as one by one the team fell asleep.

Jay jumped up quickly as Nick fell out of his jump seat and landed hard on the floor. Seconds later he was secured with flex cuffs, and then Jay and Pat went to the cockpit. The crew was just nodding off. Pat motioned to Jay to help her remove the pilot from his seat, and she settled in. Taking control of the aircraft, she smiled; it was damn good to be back in the driver's seat. Jay removed the co-pilot and navigator and dragged them to the rear of the plane. All three were lined up, sleeping and ready to go. He returned to the cockpit and motioned that they were ready. Pat opened a radio channel and began:

"Mayday, mayday, mayday, this is flight…" she continued as she pushed the nose of the plane abruptly downward, toward the ocean. It would take no small amount of skill to know exactly when to pull up. The plane had to level out just above the water. Too low, and they all die; too high, and it won't look right.

At what she hoped was the right altitude, she leveled off. *Excellent guess*, she complimented herself.

As the plane leveled off, Jay was dumping the flight crew out the rear cargo door into the dark, cold water. Next came the aircraft parts and the garbage, and then he dumped two fifty-gallon drums of JP-8 into the ocean as well. For that special added touch, he'd removed articles of clothing from each of the tactical team members before he secured them all with flex cuffs. A shirt here, boot there, items to make the crash site look legit. All went out the cargo door into the nighttime waters of the ocean. Once he was done, he closed the door and secured it. Walking back towards the front of the craft, he realized he had to piss. A sly smirk came to his face, and he walked over to where Nick was lying restrained on the floor.

No better time than the present, he thought and began to empty his considerably full bladder into Nick's face. Smiling, he couldn't remember the last time taking a piss felt so damn good. To add to his sadistic pleasure, Nick actually turned his face up into the steaming stream. This was too good to be true; the cocky bastard actually liked the golden shower.

When Jay had finished with Nick, he crossed the plane to where Nõn was seated, hanging like a rag doll from the four point restraints of the jump seat. He dropped her onto the floor as well and restrained her arms and legs. He returned to the cockpit and motioned to Pat that it went well, the parts and bodies were in the ocean. She signaled a thumbs up and smiled. Jay was the kind of guy she could work with. Like her, he saw the bigger picture. Better to be a wolf than a sheep. Wolves survived. She saw herself as an observer, someone who stood in the eye of the hurricane and watched the chaos she created but was unaffected by it. She liked that feeling of detachment. It was comforting.

She flew on into the night; in another hour, she'd entered the Darien Gap. Soon after, she was circling Sambu Airfield. This was the easiest money she'd made in a long time.

Once they'd touched down on the airfield, they taxied to two waiting vehicles. Pat shut down the engines and completed the necessary checklists. Her instructions were clear; they planned on using the aircraft for future missions, so she had to take care of it. There was a future here for her, if all went according to plan. That was exactly what she wanted to hear. Once she was done, she went to the back of the plane and began the difficult process of unloading the equipment and still drugged tactical team, Nick and Nõn.

Pat had to admit, Jay had thought of everything. To remove the eight bodies of the team, he'd come up with the idea of using upright furniture dollies. Each team member was tied to a dollie and rolled off the plane with very little effort.

She smiled a yellow-toothed grin at Jay and said, "You watched Silence of the Lambs, I see. I loved that part where Lecter torments the senator."

Jay laughed and replied, "It seemed to be a simple solution to the problem of loading, and it works!"

In no time, all of the people and equipment had been removed from the plane and secured in the two military surplus deuce and a half cargo trucks that had been waiting for their arrival. Jay left with the vehicles. Pat's part in the mission was complete. She would now meet with her ride back to the states. The boat was supposed to arrive in one hour at a dock on the Atlantic side of the Darien Gap. From there it would be a nice, leisurely trip back to the Gulf of Mexico, and then home. Sipping mango flavored daiquiris the entire way is how she'd imagined the trip. She loved being recognized for just how unique she really was. Hopefully, they would need her services again soon.

After loading the team onto the truck, Jay jumped into the truck and began the bumpy journey to "Baroota." He still had a lot of preparations left to do. He had two weeks to facilitate the mission: one week for the clients to complete their hunt, and one week to clean up the mess. Then it would be back to the states.

BAROOTA

It had been 10 years since Jay had been on the safari in South Africa. Following his guide into the African savannah, he'd been promised a shot at an African lion. He scoffed as the guide guaranteed he would be taking his long awaited shot at his dream trophy kill. Two hours and one shot later, he was standing over his trophy African lion. It was almost too easy. He asked the guide how he had could have possibly been able to know for sure where the lion would be. At first the guide had refused to tell, but Jay had been persistent, and even the alcohol didn't loosen the tongue of the guide.

Finally, Jay just gave up. Going back to his tent, he thought about the day; it had been hot, and dry. South Africa had been in the midst of another drought. Jay hadn't seen much wildlife since he'd been in country. Every single species was hunkered down and just trying to survive the drought. As Jay slipped off to sleep, it came to him. The guide knew not only the area, but he'd studied the patterns of the animals. Bottom line, they had to have water! Simple as that. Every animal needed water, and the lions knew that as well; instinctively, the lion knew its prey needed water. The guide knew the lions were waiting for their prey at the water, and being the apex hunter, they didn't expect that knowledge to be used against them. That was their weakness. They were as dependent on the water for survival as the animals they hunted.

The next day, Jay told the guide he'd solved the riddle. It was the water, right? The guide smiled and said nothing. Jay knew he'd figured out the secret. Once you understood your prey and its strengths, you also knew its weaknesses. He never forgot that lesson.

This new perspective had changed his perception of his enemies. He no longer saw their strengths as only strengths; he realized now they were simultaneously weaknesses as well. They formed a pattern of behavior that could be exploited, guided and manipulated. At work, armed with this knowledge he became a better hunter of his ultimate prey. Man.

His military career enabled him to sharpen those skills, and eventually his military successes came to the attention of the director.

It didn't take much convincing from the director to get Jay on board for his "little project," as he called it. The recent events worldwide had created a lot of potential customers for the project. People who were motivated to perhaps even the score against the no-name faces of military personnel who had invaded their countries en masse. Crimes were always committed in warfare. It was the nature of the beast. This created a market the director was keen to take advantage of. It was just good business, really. He provided a service where none existed before. He just waited for the perfect moment and then dropped a suggestion in the ear of an angry, wealthy father of a recent victim of a "signature drone strike." That was eight years ago, and several successful hunts at "Baroota".

Of course, there had been bugs to work out. For the most part, all the hunts had been profitable, and the word had quietly been passed around the dark circles of those few elite people who had been wronged by the winds of war. Wronged, and yet had the power and money to survive those very same winds, and they wanted vengeance.

Jay had been useful to the director. He'd been told to chose a location that was remote enough to be of practical use, and yet not so far as to be financially unfeasible. Jay immediately suggested the Darien Gap for the project. There were very few locations in the world that were still remote and untouched modern technologies. He'd supervised the construction of facilities at Baroota and had even named the compound after a short trip to the outback of Australia.

Jay had chosen a simple design for the home base of Baroota. It was a military design that was simple and had clean lines. It was functional and very basic. There were three main buildings, at the southernmost end of the home base. One was the command center, the other a multi-purpose building that served whatever need was required. Some days it was used to brief the incoming clients of the rules of the hunt; others it was used to celebrate another successful completion of a mission. The third building was a storage area, where the trophies were kept until their sponsors arrived. Behind the three main buildings were twelve small "huts". Arranged in two rows of six huts each, they were actually large metal shipping containers that had been remodeled into small luxury cabins for the clients. They were secure, clean and buried under a mound of dirt, which surrounded the containers on all sides except the doorway. After six months in the Darien Gap, the containers had become invisible to any imagery taken from above. The local fauna had completely covered them. The only visible buildings from above were the three main buildings and the support equipment. A large diesel generator provided power to the camp, and water was obtained from local sources. At one end of the compound was a diesel-powered wood chipper.

To Jay, the camp was a reminder of military function and form at its best. Everything had a place and purpose. Squared, flush and grounded. The design appealed to his need to be in control and never, ever be surprised. Jay didn't like surprises. To be surprised meant you hadn't prepared adequately. To Jay, it meant failure. True success could only be achieved by being in control at all times. Both in his professional life and his personal life, Jay liked being in control. He never bounced a check, never received a parking ticket. He liked his coffee hot and his life orderly, his women submissive.

The Darien Gap is home to one of the most primitive people in the world, the Wounaan. The Wounaan were initially suspicious of Jay because they believed he was affiliated with the illegal logging crews that had been harvesting the forests and destroying their lands. Jay found them to be a simple people who wished for nothing more than to be left alone. They wanted nothing to do with the outside world. Years of dealing with narcotics traffickers and gunrunners had made them suspicious of the outside world. People outside the gap seemed to them to be filled with insanity and greed.

It took many attempts to negotiate with the tribal leaders before Jay was successful in negotiating and securing a couple men for labor around the camp. He explained he would provide the men with training, uniforms and supplies for their village if they would simply protect the camp and keep their mouths shut about the activities at Baroota. He needed guides that were dependable and trustworthy. For that, he would pay generously. He also hinted he had a surefire method of dealing with the logging crews, which turned out to be brutally effective. Jay secured a deal with the Wounaan leaders after demonstrating his sincere brutality in dealing with the loggers. He wanted them in the area of the Darien Gap even less than the Wounaan, but for much different reasons. Soon it was clear to the logging crews: leave the gap in peace, or face the wrath of the jungle people. Afterwards, Jay was a welcome face among the Wounaan. He explained he would return from time to time to keep up with the infestation of the logging crews, and occasionally he would bring others who would help. Strangers from far away who wish to protect the gap and the Wounaan. It was a ruse, but it explained to the Wounaan the occasional hunting parties' arrival in the gap. The prey they hunted would be explained away as overzealous loggers who needed to be reminded of their place in the Wounaan's jungle. The unsuspecting Wounaan welcomed the hunts, and their problems were solved.

The first hunt had been a challenge for Jay. He had no idea what to expect from anyone involved. He tried to anticipate any possible problem and then take preventative measures to deal with that problem. Running through several different scenarios in his head, playing devil's advocate, he was able to have preventative measures in place for nearly every contingency. From that hunt, he realized he needed to have clearly defined rules for the sponsors. If they didn't follow the rules, they were out and on their way back home. Things had gone south with one sponsor, and they'd wanted a little extra vengeance than the hunts allowed for. Extra vengeance wasn't the problem; that was the point of the hunts, but it had to be planned for and organized. Jay was a professional, and the sloppy results of the day's events on that particular hunt had made it clear to him, rules needed to be in place and respected by the sponsors.

Jay arrived back in Baroota with the team, Nick and Nõn. He and the two drivers unloaded the equipment the team had packed for their mission. What the team didn't know as they packed was they were each packing their individual sponsors' gift bags. Personal mementos of the hunt. Each sponsor would be given the equipment used by their chosen prey, provided they followed the rules of the camp and dispatched their chosen trophy within the confines of those rules. It had been an obvious benefit that had come to him after the first hunt, when one of the sponsors had requested the weapon used by his trophy kill. Jay had an epiphany at that moment, and after discussing it with the director, they had agreed to provide the token mementos at an additional price. Since then, every single sponsor had paid the extra cost for the equipment. It made the whole operation at Baroota more efficient, tidy and orderly. Jay especially liked that aspect, the efficiency of the whole operation.

Once the equipment was unloaded, the dollies were rolled into the third building. The team would need to be inspected by their sponsors to ensure that they met the specifications agreed to in the initial contract. Some wanted their trophies to know who they were and why they'd been chosen for the hunt, others wanted to remain anonymous. This required specific details to be followed for each individual case. For this particular hunt, all of the trophies would be brought out of the warehouse and placed around the campfire, where they would be introduced to their sponsors. The intention of the next day's events would be detailed to the trophies, and then they would be wheeled back into the warehouse. Understandably, some of the trophies would break down, some evacuated their bowels, some cried, others said nothing. On one particular hunt, a trophy had refused to move at all after being released.

That had been the hunt that had been messy, and new rules had to be put in place.

Until the hunt was complete, every detail of the plan would be followed to the letter. Water and food were withheld from the trophies; the idea was to make their behavior as predictable as possible. Thirst and hunger were basic survival needs; once the trophies were released, they would focus on those needs immediately. The plan had been perfected until the trophy's behavior could be predicted to the letter. It made the whole operation cleaner and more professional in Jay's mind. It also sped up the hunts, which made the sponsors happy. The environment of the Darien Gap was less than comfortable. It was one of the most remote and wild regions of the world. The quicker the hunts were complete, the happier the clients.

Nõn awoke as they were wheeling Nick off the truck. She remembered the feeling of being drugged from her childhood. She had avoided any drug or alcohol from the time of her childhood, simply because she understood how helpless you could be once you were under another person's control and drugged. You were completely at their mercy. Nõn pretended to be still unconscious as they came for her next and wheeled her to the building where she and the others would be held. She hoped by playing her own ruse, she might gain some insight into what was going on and how to possibly escape. Obviously, something had gone wrong. Now she had to figure out what was going on and who, if anyone, she could trust.

Once the entire team had been offloaded and secured in the building, they were left alone. Time was needed to allow hunger and thirst to set in. The drug they had been given had been chosen for several reasons. One, it worked. It worked on everyone, every single time. Drug addiction and tolerances built up by alcohol abuse had no impact on its effectiveness. Everyone went down once they drank the tainted water. The next benefit it had was it made the trophies extremely thirsty; near panic had occurred in some of the trophies, their thirst was so extreme. And the final benefit: it impaired their cognitive abilities. Hunger and thirst became a priority no one could ignore. It made the trophies much more manageable.

The sponsors had arrived by plane as well and had landed at Sambu airfield in their own privately owned aircraft. Sambu had been chosen as the landing site because it was one of the few runways in the area that had been paved. It could accommodate the sponsors' aircraft. Once the sponsors had arrived and had taken up residence in their assigned living quarters, they were given basic meals and water. The point of their trip was about to become a reality. Jay informed each of them there would be a briefing at 1800 hours, and then if there were no questions, they would meet their trophies. The hunt would begin the next morning.

The building in which Nõn, Nick and the tactical team was being housed was referred to as the trophy room by Jay and the two workers he employed. After being dropped off there, the trophies had been left alone. One by one, they started to wake up and realize something was very wrong. They started talking to each other and trying to piece together what exactly had happened. Being the team leader, Rooney tried to establish some kind of order; he reasserted his leadership role and began with a pep talk to the team. He reminded them that their best chances of defeating whatever plan Jay had really had for them was as a team, working together against a common foe.

"We've been in some bad places as a team before," he reminded them, "and we came through it as a unit. We can deal with this as well."

Nick noticed the not so subtle exclusion of him and Nõn from the discussion. It was clear to him in a survival setting, they were on their own. There would be no help from the "zero dark thirty" team.

"So what's the plan, Rooney? What do we do next?" asked Rohlk.

Rooney explained he had no plan; there was not enough information to know what to do. Jay had told them nothing. They'd been dumped in the trophy room and left. No one even knew yet for sure that Jay was involved, much less responsible for their circumstances.

Nõn interrupted. "Jay is a part of this. I was awake before the rest of you. I pretended to be unconscious, but I was awake. We are in serious trouble."

Green replied, "Did you overhear anything at all?"

Nõn said, "No, not much. We were loaded onto these dollies and then driven here by truck. There was not a lot of conversation between the people who loaded us."

Rooney asked, "How many did you see?"

Nõn replied, "Only three, Jay and two others, workers that helped him load us onto the trucks. There was a third, a woman, but it seemed like she was leaving. It was hard to tell; I was still very much under the drug's influence."

Rooney asked, "Does anyone know how we were drugged?"

No one said anything, then finally Nick spoke. "It was the water. It had to be. I remember wondering why Jay didn't get a bottle during that last round the loadmaster passed around. She made a point of not offering Jay a bottle. That was the only variation I noticed."

Rooney replied, "Any idea what the hell is going on, Nick? You're the one who's here to think outside the box. What the hell is this shit?"

Nõn interrupted, "I think we have been duped, that is obvious. If they wanted us dead immediately, we would have been. You notice the aircrew is not here. I don't know what happened to them or if they are a part of this, but my feeling is they are dead. That means we are alive for a reason. Where I came from, people are drugged to be moved, managed, bought and sold. I would imagine whatever the plan is for us, as a group we are alive because they need us to be. When they no longer need us to be alive, we will be killed. It is simple."

Johnson erupted, "Screw that shit, what the hell do you know, bitch? How do we know you aren't one of them, planted here to fuck with our heads? This might be one big mental fucking game to test our loyalty to this mission. Anyone thought of that?" The room was quiet as the team contemplated the idea.

Nick stepped in. "You're right, man; they just drugged you, tied you to a dollie, and rolled you in here to test your loyalty. Makes perfect sense to me, just be a good, loyal soldier boy, and everything will be okie dokie. Can you say halleluiah? Praise Jesus? No worries, Johnson, you will be saved! Jesus loves you, man!"

A heated round of insults were exchanged between Nick and the team as Nõn rolled her eyes; sometimes Nick could be such an ass. The sarcastic humor was obviously a coping mechanism. He knew, as did she, they were in a very precarious situation. But angering the team did nothing to help them. It just further cemented the idea that they weren't a part of the group. Not part of the team. They all needed each other now.

Jay opened the door to the trophy room and walked in as the team and Nick were just starting to get warmed up for round two of who really could insult the other the best. So far, Nõn thought it was a draw and had accomplished nothing.

Jay began speaking. "Gentlemen, the time has come to listen, and listen carefully. In a couple of hours, you will be wheeled out of this building and placed around a large bonfire. There, you will meet your sponsors. These are men who have spent a great deal of money, time and effort to bring you all here today. Most of you will not know who your sponsors are. You have never met, but you have had a huge impact on their lives, and they wish to return the favor. Do you have any questions?"

Rooney spoke, "What the fuck is this, Jay? What about our agreement? What about the mission? Explain yourself, motherfucker!"

Nick rolled his eyes; these guys were still trying to make this about a mission, an agreement. Their structured thinking could not wrap their heads around the fact that they'd been duped.

Jay smiled and only said, "Welcome to Camp Baroota, gentlemen and woman," and left the building.

The team erupted as near seizure-like violence rolled through them. They fought against their restraints and screamed violent threats at the door Jay had departed through. This went on at this pace for at least half an hour before they slowly came back down. Nick watched and wondered what they hoped to accomplish. If they could have escaped, they would have already. Pointless effort was just that: pointless. Now was the time to conserve energy and wait for the moment to strike.

Finally someone said, "Damn, I'm thirsty. I mean, like, I really need a drink of water." It was a comment they all agreed with, and by morning it would be expressed in panicked voices. The drug was doing its job.

CHAPTER 15

Taking their seats, the sponsors nodded to one another. They each were here for one reason. No one spoke about it, but it was understood. They were here to right the wrongs that had been done to them, to regain control of their lives and extract vengeance on those who had harmed them. Right and wrong were no longer the issue, if they ever had been. Anyone who lives in the real world knows there is no right and wrong, not really. Nations may spin the story to justify their actions, but for the victims of those actions there was no right and wrong. It was all wrong; the only difference between those who victimized and those who were victims was strength. The strong won, the weak were subjugated. It was simple as that. This was the mindset of the people in the room.

Jay entered the room and walked to the front of the small group of hunters. Smiling, he began his well-rehearsed speech.

"Gentlemen, welcome to Camp Baroota. Let's get started. In one hour, you will meet the trophy you have selected to hunt during your stay here. Before we begin, you must understand and agree to a specific set of rules and guidelines. There will be no tolerance of any kind for breaking these rules. They are set in place for several reasons. They are in place for your protection. This is not our first hunt, and it won't be our last. These rules are non-negotiable. Are there any questions?"

There were none.

"Excellent. First rule is, you will follow your guides' instructions. They are experienced in the local customs, and they are familiar with the local area. They will keep you safe if you follow their directions.

"Second, you will draw straws to determine who goes first in the hunt. Straws cannot be exchanged. Where you draw is where you draw. This hunt is not an ego contest. At the successful completion of your hunt, you will be given the trophies' possessions if you have purchased them and be taken to the airport to begin your journey home. The record for the fastest successful hunt is 4 hours, beginning to end. We encourage you to try to break that record. Once the first hunt has ended, the next hunt will begin.

"Third. There will be no night hunts. If your trophy survives the first day, you will start over the next day. Don't worry; that has never happened in any of our hunts. The guides are that skilled in their craft.

"Fourth. Do not, and I cannot emphasize this enough, DO NOT engage the local indigenous people. We are their guests, after several years of negotiations, they have allowed us to maintain the camp and conduct our business unmolested. Leave them alone. Is that clear?"

Everyone nodded in agreement.

"Excellent, are there any questions?"

One man raised his voice and said, "I don't care about all of this bullshit, when do I meet the bitch?"

Jay flushed with anger; there was always one who thought he was above the rules and wanted to be top dog. One who felt they came first. He supposed it was the nature of the clientele. Powerful people thought the rules didn't concern them, they weren't patient and saw nothing wrong with their arrogance.

Jay dodged the question and simply replied to the entire group, "In less than one hour, you will be face to face with your trophy.

"Now, a little history and some facts about Camp Baroota. The camp is approximately 100 square miles in width and length, in the middle of the Darien Gap. The Darien Gap is one of the most remote locations in the world. There are several indigenous tribes that live here and allow us to conduct our business. The average rainfall in the area is 1728 mm. There are 101 days of rain. So plan on getting wet." Jay continued on with random facts and figures no one really cared about. The group had a single-minded purpose: The Hunt.

Finally, Jay left the room, glaring at the man who had challenged him but maintaining a professional demeanor as he walked out. In one week it would be complete, and then the clean up would begin. In two weeks he would be home, and rich.

After the briefing of the sponsors, Jay and the two workers returned to the trophy room. They began the process of cutting off and removing the clothing of everyone in the room. Boots, shirts, pants, socks, all removed until everyone was left nude, still strapped to their dollie. Green spit in one of the workers' faces and received a quick, deep cut with a box cutter across his left arm. The intended message was clear.

The two workers gathered the now shredded clothing and removed it from the trophy room, taking it out to where the bonfire was just being lit.

Once the door closed behind them, the intended effect of removing the trophies' clothing began to settle in. Psychologically, it changed everything for their mindset. The team had been wearing uniforms, different from Nick and Nōn; they identified with the clothing that had been shredded and removed from them. Removing the uniforms stripped them of their identity and unity. Each of them had worn some kind of uniform for the past ten years, both in the military and out.

For Nick and Nōn, the impact on their psyche was less damaging. Nōn had worn long-sleeved, heavy cotton clothing for a reason. That reason was now clear. She was covered with thick, rope-like scars. The scars crossed her torso and legs in a woven pattern similar to a wicker basket or chair. Everyone in the trophy room saw the scars, but no one commented. It was clear now Nōn had been tortured extensively. Nick realized this explained the texture under Nōn's shirt he'd felt on the bus when he'd put his arm around her. It wasn't a vest under her shirt; it was scarring like he had no idea was possible.

Nōn waited for the questions about her scars to begin, her head down, thinking. Who would want her dead? She had no enemies, no one who hated her this much, enough to hunt her, kill her. The questions never came, the team was too demoralized from the removal of their clothing and cognitively impaired by the drug. Nōn was grateful for the silence. It helped her think.

The trophies were brought out and placed in a circle around the fire. As they waited, their clothing was thrown into the fire. The effect on them was exactly what Jay had intended. He'd left nothing to chance. The symbolism of their burning clothes was clear, there would be no escape, this was no test of loyalty, as Johnson had foolishly hoped.

Once the trophies were in place around the fire, the sponsors were brought out. Jay began the meeting with his favorite quote from Sun Tzu.

"Gentlemen, the great Sun Tzu is quoted as saying, 'The supreme art of war is to subdue your enemy without fighting.' Today, we have done exactly that for all of you."

Nick noticed a subtle but definite grouping of the team apart from himself and Nõn. Whatever they were here for, they had done as a group. He had no idea who he could have possibly pissed off this much; the list was too long to bother trying to figure out. Besides, soon enough he would know. Nõn, on the other hand, that was a mystery. The scars crisscrossing over her body had come from somewhere, and from someone sadistic and brutal.

Jay addressed the team first. "Gentlemen, as I'm sure all of you remember, you served in Iraq together in the small city of Umm Qasr. Your squad was in competition with another large squad in Afghanistan. That squad was based in the Afghanistan city of La Mohammed Kalay, in the province of Kandahar, and your squad was based in the Iraqi city of Umm Qasr. It has been proven beyond a reasonable doubt that your two squads hunted civilians and formed a pact to become 'kill squads'. Taking trophies and staging the evidence to protect yourselves from prosecution, you committed crimes and atrocities which were never brought to light. The La Mohammed Kalay kill squad was less successful in hiding their crimes and were court-martialed. Your crimes were never discovered by the press. They were hidden from the outside world with the Pentagon's blessing. The feeling was enough damage had been done to the United States military's image with the facts detailed in the press release of the La Mohammed Kalay killings. Today, however, you will answer for those killings. The six gentlemen in front of you have waited a long time for this meeting."

Rooney's team defiantly glared back into the eyes of the men who were their sponsors. The past had been buried for a long time, the kill squad they'd formed had been hidden from public scrutiny for so long, they actually had forgotten about its existence. They'd moved on, the families of the men killed by their squad would never move on until the debt had been paid. They'd welcomed the American and British troops as they came ashore. They'd done nothing to provoke Rooney and his men, there was no need to. The team was a perfect combination of the 'wrong stuff' for combat. The six men said nothing to Rooney's team. There was nothing to say. They'd waited a long time to even this score. The time had arrived. There was nothing but silence and hatred exchanged between the two groups for several minutes. Finally, Jay walked over to Nick and smiled.

"And you little fucking prick, I'm sure you won't recognize your sponsor. You were a pain in the ass to locate. Just sheer luck, really, that you fit the bill we were looking for. Remember that dinner at the Mash-house? You started bragging about all of your stupid accomplishments, and I realized you were the exact fit I was looking for. We had a sponsor who had no real specific target for us to acquire. He simply wanted to hunt and kill a veteran SWAT cop. You know, the whole post-Ferguson environment has stirred up a lot of resentment towards cops. Your sponsor just wanted to be able to kill one of you, for no other reason than just to do it. Congratulations, dickweed, you won the lottery."

A soft, middle-aged man stepped forward and smiled. "Hello, Nick, sorry for the inconvenience. I've read your resume, and it's most impressive. I hope you'll be able to live up to my expectations. I expect this to be a most rewarding experience. I've wondered what it would be like to kill someone like you for a long time. Finally, I'll get the opportunity." The man had a constant smile on his face that instantly irritated Nick.

Nick sized-up the soft, middle-aged man in front of him up. "I'm guessing you spend a lot of time fantasizing about a lot of sick shit, am I right?" The soft, fat man started to fidget uncomfortably as Nick continued to berate and humiliate him. Finally, Nick struck a nerve. "How many children have you molested, you sick, fat fuck? Be honest, ten, maybe more? I can see it in your eyes, I'm right!"

His sponsor lost it and screamed at Nick, "You will learn to respect me, soon enough. I own your ass, and I will see you suffer. I've paid a lot of money to see you suffer!" He screamed this at Nick.

"Don't hold your baby-raping breath, bitch," Nick responded. He watched the fat lump of shit struggle with his emotions. This wasn't what he'd hoped for. He wanted Nick to beg for his life. Plead with him to spare him. Instead, Nick had ridiculed him and somehow known his darkest, deepest secret. He was indeed a pedophile.

"Tell me your name, you fat bag of shit, at least that way maybe I can fulfill your last sick fantasy and beg you for forgiveness at the very end."

His sponsor took the bait and smiled a satisfied, content smile.

"My name is Kerry."

"Is that K-e-r-r-y, or C-a-r-r-i-e? I'm guessing you prefer the C-a-r-r-i-e, am I right, you candy ass fuck?"

Kerry was beside himself with rage. Spitting fury at Nick, he yelled, "You will respect me! I am an important man! I have had a distinguished career, people look up to me!"

Kerry didn't realize Nick was just hitting his stride. He could drop insults on pathetic garbage like Kerry all day.

"People look up to the Stay Puff marshmallow man as well, you cocksucker. You've never known what real respect is. People laugh at your candy ass behind your back, trust me, with that stupid self-important smile of yours. People are always laughing at you behind your back."

Nick continued, "I bet you're even a vegetarian. God knows what meat would do to your frail ass; you might actually get a hard-on for a woman, instead of those naked little boy pictures you keep hidden in a shoebox, am I right? Sucking a carrot make you hard, li'l man?"

Kerry stomped his feet in a rage-filled tantrum, clenching and unclenching his fists as a weird, sick, high-pitched whine erupted from deep within his chest while Nick continued.

Nõn watched the exchange between Nick and his sponsor carefully. Somewhere in the exchange, she'd become lost in the realization that she was staring at the tattoo on Nick's left shoulder. Experiencing tunnel vision. She'd nearly forgotten her dream in the chaotic hurricane of events that had occurred in the last twenty-four hours. The intensity of her focus was broken only by the toxicity of a familiar voice from her unpleasant past. Nõn jumped as she was startled back to the present, her reality rudely assaulted by the venom in the thick accent of that familiar voice.

"There you are, you worthless little excuse for a whore."

Nõn hadn't spoken his name since that night in the hut, motioning to the bleeding girl to leave. She'd refused to speak it. He was dead in her mind.

"Nõnkos Zia," he continued, "do you remember me? You should, I used to fuck you when I had no others to use. You were by far my least favorite. Do you remember how you used to lay there when I was through with you? Unemotional, like a limp rag doll? I do, I've looked forward to this day for a very long time. When I'm done with you, you will feel pain like you never imagined possible, you will scream for mercy, that is a promise."

Nõn said nothing; she wouldn't allow this demon to have the satisfaction of interaction with her. She just stared, unafraid and unemotional. Her protector had shown her a sign in her dream, the wolf waiting for her in the three pyramids. Follow the wolf, that was her path. The rest would be what it would be, death was just the final act of life, she had no fear of death.

Her sponsor wanted something from her, some sign of fear or anger. Some emotion, any emotion. Instead, she was exactly as he remembered her when he raped her, unemotional, barely present in this world. He wanted to see her fear of him, instead she refused to acknowledge him. It drove him insane with rage, much like Nick's taunting of the soft, fat, and ever smiling pedophile.

The meeting was over, the sponsors watched as the naked trophies were wheeled back to the trophy room, and then they went back to their own individual huts and waited for the hunt to begin in the morning.

CHAPTER 16

Back inside the trophy room, no one said a word for several minutes. The team's darkest secret was out, and their demeanor changed in kind. The façade of the uniform and the hope of this being some kind of loyalty test removed, the team began to display exactly what Nick had realized the night of the pushup contest. They were no better than the human traffickers they'd been duped into being hired to hunt. Nick had to give Jay credit, he'd played his hand with each and every one of them expertly.

Rooney broke the silence. "So now you know why our asses are here. I'm sorry, Nick, but I couldn't hear what the paper pusher Pillsbury Doughboy had to say to you. Why would he want to hunt you? Did you steal his favorite 6th grade lay from him?"

"You nailed it, Rooney, I had better Legos and stole his boy toy for my own sick use. Now he wants payback."

Rooney laughed. "No, really, what the hell does he want with you?"

Nick was more serious now. "Guess I won the lottery, seems the sick prick is a sadist. He likes to torture and molest small children and has some sick fantasy in which I end up begging him for my life. He's never met me before today and has no idea who I am. I just fit the pedigree he was looking for. That's all. Trust me, if I get the chance, he'll regret this decision. He has no idea of the shit storm coming his way."

No one said a word. They all knew talk was cheap. Naked and tied to the dollies, it was easy to brag about what you would do when you were freed. Reality was, they were all at their sponsors' mercy.

The team made small talk with each other for the next couple of hours, tossing contingencies back and forth, what to do if this happened or that happened.

Finally, Rohlk said to Nõn, "So who was that tall black dude? He looked really pissed at you, Nõn. An old boyfriend, maybe?"

Everyone on the team laughed.

Nick watched Nõn as she took a deep breath. As she began to tell the story of who her sponsor was, the room was instantly silent as all the men realized her voice had changed and she now spoke with a thick accent.

"When I was a girl, I went through an unfortunate series of events. I thought I had escaped the local medicine man who was trying to harvest my body. My red hair makes certain parts of my body more magically powerful to medicine men, and they will pay a high price for the breasts or labia of a virgin redhead. You see, in my village only my brother and I were redheads, and we were hunted by those who practice Muti medicine. The hunters killed my brother and cut his body up to sell to the Muti medicine men. I escaped, or so I had thought at first. I was taken in by a woman who I thought was kind, and she treated me well. Instead, she sold me to human traffickers. I was sold as a sex slave, and to make the whole story shorter, I ended up as the property of that demon you saw today. I learned early on that he liked to see others in pain, he enjoyed it. Later, I realized he was a pure sadist. He could only enjoy raping me if I reacted. I learned to escape into my head and gave him nothing to enjoy. I think the mechanism is called Dissociative Disorder. It felt like I left my body and went somewhere else."

The room was quiet for several minutes while the team waited, realizing now the hell Nõn had been raised in. She continued quietly.

"He would beat me repeatedly with a long piece of wire, whipping me for hours at a time. He wanted to see me cry, to hear me beg for him to stop. I did neither. I would not give him the reward for his efforts. I realized it took his power over me away by refusing to cry out. I should have died many times, but I did not. One night I awoke and felt I was ready to die, and I somehow knew that he had planned on killing me since I refused to please him. I was very weak from the beatings, my wounds were infected, and I actually welcomed death. Then I was visited by my protector. My name was taken from a woman who was a prophet of sorts among my people many years before I was born. She guided and protected my people in a time of great pain and many wars. My protector came to me in a dream and told me to take my tormentor's power, I was filled with her strength. I felt healed, strong and fearless. I walked through the camp weaving among my captors, who were now asleep and drunk. I walked to his cabin and found a young girl there bleeding, crying. He had finished with her and had fallen asleep. I motioned to her to be silent and leave, which she did. I tied him up with the ropes he had bound the young girl with and took his power."

Garcia rolled his eyes. "What the hell does that mean, took his power? Like what, you took his Indiana Jones whip? What the does that mean, Nõn?"

Nõn looked at Garcia, her eyes now dark and cold. "The demon had a pet hyena he kept tied up in the camp. I tied the demon up, and piece by piece I cut off his power and fed it to the hyena. The demon screamed while he watched me feed his power to the hyena. But I had bound him and stuffed his mouth with rags. No one could hear his screams. I wanted him to know his torture of children was ending. Piece by piece, it was ending. When there was nothing left, I got up and began walking. It was remarkable, really. I was filled with strength and walked for miles. I should have been dead, I was so weak, but somehow my protector had filled me with strength."

Johnson, in a sarcastic tone, asked, "So what did you feed the hyena? I mean, what did you think was his power?"

Nick interrupted, "She cut off his dick, you idiot, piece by piece she cut off his cock and fed it to his pet hyena. Her demon had hurt the kids with his dick, so she took it from him."

Nõn replied, "Yes, exactly," looking at Nick with a strange look. No one she'd ever dared to tell the story to had understood what Nick had immediately. Again she could see the tattoo on his shoulder and stared at it. She couldn't see his face, as he was always placed facing away from her towards the outside wall of the room. They all faced outward in the room, so they only caught a sideways glimpse of each other as they talked.

The team was silent for some time, finally someone whispered quietly, "Holy hell, that shit is brutal. Remind me not to piss that bitch off."

Nõn broke her silence. "Nick, what is that design on your shoulder? Does it have any meaning?"

Nick mumbled, "Which shoulder? They both have tattoos. I have tattoos all over."

She replied, "The geometric design on your left shoulder, surrounded by a circle."

"Oh, that one. The circle is a Chaos star, it's a Viking symbol. Its eight points symbolize the potential for chaos in any decision. Some see it as satanic, but it was originally intended to mean unlimited possibilities were present at every decision. Inside the star is the shape of a Valknut, it's a warrior's symbol that represents the nine worlds of the Vikings' mythology. Each world was basically a level of existence. The Viking beliefs are complex. The warrior's goal was to die well in battle and reach Valhalla."

Nõn's vision narrowed, the room became very dark. All she could see was the tattoo of the three interlocking triangles. The Valknut, as he'd called it, looked like three pyramids interwoven. Nõn felt herself slipping slowly into unconsciousness and was barely aware of her own voice asking, "What are the other tattoos you have?"

The last thing she heard before the darkness came was Nick's voice saying, "I have a tattoo of a wolf head on my chest."

Nõn was unaware of the rest of the conversation in the room.

Rooney interjected, "I once knew this girl who had a ruler tattooed on her leg, beneath it said 'you must be this long to ride my ride.'"

The team erupted in laughter.

Garcia, laughing, said, "And I bet you were too damn short!"

Even louder laughter rolled out of the team. Nick had to admit, it did feel good to laugh again, even if only for a moment. Straining to look over at Nõn, he saw that her head was down and she appeared to be asleep.

One by one, they all drifted off to sleep. Fatigue had taken its toll on all of them. An hour later, Nick woke up to Rooney talking quietly to his team.

"We'll do what we did in the desert. We'll put these animals in their place. Never forget, they aren't people, they're animals, and we can defeat them. We're smarter than them, better than them."

A quiet "WHoo-Rah" rolled around the room.

Nick sighed. "Jesus, you stupid fucks will never learn, will you?"

Rooney said to Nick, "Fuck off, old man, we'll see who comes out of this alive. We survive as a team. We have each other. What do you have besides a crazy bitch who feeds dick to hyenas?"

Straining to see each other, Nick and Rooney locked eyes. Rooney was defiant to the last, sure of his ability to overcome this circumstance he and his team had found themselves in. They'd never known failure as a team. Problem was, they weren't taken out as a team. Jay had already thought of that. They were to be removed in pairs.

The next morning came much too quickly, the door opened, and Jay entered the room. "Judgment day, gentlemen." He motioned to his workers to wheel out Rooney and Rohlk. The door closed as the team shouted encouragement to the exiting team members.

Jay noticed that Nōn's head was down and slapped her face until she woke up.

Nick asked Jay for water, saying, "We're no good to your clients dead, Jay. We need at least some water; not asking for a shower and a hand job, just a bottle of water."

Jay said nothing but returned a short time later with two bottles of water. He poured a small amount into each of their mouths. Surprisingly, no one spit it back in his face; they were too thirsty to waste the water with a meaningless gesture of spite.

The next two hours passed much too quickly. The door opened to Jay's smiling face. "Gentlemen, we have a new camp record! That was the single fastest successful hunt in camp history. Rooney and Rohlk were dispatched in under two hours."

The remaining team members were rabid with rage, screaming barely comprehensible insults. They never imagined the two veterans of the Gulf War would be dispatched so quickly. They'd hoped the two would return and lead them out of this nightmare; it wouldn't come to pass. Jay motioned to his workers to remove Garcia and Johnson. They were wheeled out, and the door shut.

Outside, the scene was a grim reminder of the sins in the team's past. The sponsors were taking photos with their now deceased trophies, the lifeless bodies of Rooney and Rohlk. Trophies were also taken, and then the bodies of the former members of the hated and feared Kill Squad of Umm Qasr were dragged to the rear of the compound. The scene was a mirror of the events that had occurred in Iraq. Jay had staged it masterfully to please his clients.

Garcia and Johnson were loaded onto the still idling truck and driven deep into the jungles of the Darien Gap. A few miles away, they were removed at gunpoint and given the filthy uniform worn by loggers from a logging company that had been unfortunate enough to become the example Jay had needed to win the Wounaan tribe's loyalty. He kept the ruse alive by dressing his trophies in the logging company's uniforms. When the trophies were hunted by their sponsors, they would be stalked wearing the familiar uniforms. This served two purposes. First, it maintained the façade that Jay was protecting the Wounaan people. Second, it made it very clear to the sponsors who to shoot. Killing a Wounaan tribe member by mistake would be very problematic. The Wounaan were primitive but formidable. Jay didn't want them as enemies.

Garcia and Johnson dressed at gunpoint and then were given an empty canteen, a knife and a map of the area. Jay continued to play his twisted mind games with the trophies as he said, "Good luck, gentlemen, I hope you make a better show of it than your previous two members did. A new record! Imagine! Good luck," Jay yelled out as he drove off, headed towards the camp.

Garcia said, "Jesus, I would love to cut that smug motherfucker's throat!"

The two men headed off into the jungle using the maps. They decided to travel directly to the nearest water supply and fill the canteens. Then they would begin to plan their escape from the Darien Gap. Their plan was precisely what Jay had hoped they would do. His safari experience had been proven accurate time and time again. The trophies' pattern of behavior was incredibly predictable. Just like his lion so many years ago.

Back in the trophy room, Nick was trying to get the remaining team members to listen to him.

"Listen, whatever Rooney and Rohlk did, Jay must have anticipated it. So when we get out there, we have to think outside the box, do the unexpected. Whatever seems to be the smart thing to do, do the exact opposite. Does that make sense?"

No one responded; they were all too discouraged. They listened, but he wasn't sure how much they actually valued what he said. Even Nõn seemed lethargic.

This was no time to give up; he had to make them realize as long as they were breathing, they could fight back. They may not win, but they could fight. His words of encouragement fell on deaf and defeated ears.

Four hours later, the door opened. Jay walked in quietly. Looking at the curious faces, he said nothing, toying with the group. Finally, he said, "Garcia and Johnson are dead. They lasted longer than the first two, but still four hours, gentlemen? I expected more from the famous Kill Squad of Umm Qasr. Sad, really, but I must admit, my clients are extremely happy today. We'll be picking up again tomorrow where we left off. Sleep well, goodnight." Jay left the trophy room and secured the door.

Outside, Nick could hear the celebration as the sponsors celebrated their day of vengeance. Inside the trophy room, there was now little hope in anyone's mind that they would survive this nightmare.

An hour later, the sound of some type of machinery pierced the air for about ten minutes. It was louder than the normal gas-powered generators that provided power for the complex. It sounded like the blade of a sawmill, laboring as it cut green wood. It wasn't. Once the machine stopped running, Nick heard the jungle come to life. He didn't like the way the animal noises sounded, frantic and hungry.

Then there was the unmistakable sound of one of the trucks' motors starting up.

Several hours later, Nick awoke to someone crying in the dark. It wasn't Nõn, he could hear her breathing to his left. He wasn't surprised it wasn't her. She'd survived a lot in her short life, that much was clear. She didn't strike him as the crying type. Fossum and Green were the only two team members left besides he and Nõn. Nick thought about trying to convince the crying team member that there was still hope, then he thought better of it and just closed his eyes. Time to prepare; he could be next in the chute. He wanted a piece of that child molesting prick before he died. He had to survive to make that happen. No way after all he'd been through in his screwed up life was he going down at the hands of a perpetually smiling, carrot sucking, candy assed pedophile with soft hands. Absolutely no way.

Once Jay had secured the trophy room, he directed the workers to clean up the camp from the day's events. He liked things to be neat and tidy, and the unexpected success of the day's hunts had caught his team off guard. In the morning, the next hunt would begin. With any luck, he might be home before the usual two weeks each hunt had previously taken. The successful sponsors were given their choice of their trophies' possessions to keep as mementos of the hunt. Once they'd chosen the trinkets, the rest of the deceased trophies' possessions were put into the nightly fire. The workers had dragged the bodies of the second successful hunt to the rear of the camp, where they'd left Rooney and Rohlk earlier. One of the workers began the arduous process of starting the heavy duty wood chipper. One by one, the men's bodies were fed into the chipper and came out the other side in a huge red cone of bone and meat, spraying into the jungle of the Darien Gap. The jungle came alive with rodents, some small, others alarmingly huge. They began to feast on the mush that now covered the jungle foliage. The rats had become a problem at first and had to be trained not to come into the camp. Traps were put out, and captured animals were tortured and then released, the idea being the memory of the torture would keep them from returning to the camp. The conditioning had worked; the rats didn't return, and the ones that had since been captured were increasingly aggressive. They knew the results of being caught wouldn't be pleasant.

Always, Jay applied the lessons of his own successful hunt so many years ago. Smiling, he remembered the last flight he'd taken just before leaving for Camp Baroota. Standing at a small convenience store in the airport, he had picked up a newspaper, hoping to catch the latest scores in the playoffs. An article had caught his eye as he scanned the paper. He laughed out loud as he read about some damn dentist who was being spotlighted. Seems the dentist had been on safari and killed a lion that was the local favorite. Now the entire world was up in arms over the death of the pet lion. Jay laughed at the irony of the situation.

Jay loaded the gear of the day's successful sponsors and prepared to take them to the airport. They would leave tonight. Jay liked his hunts to be conducted by the numbers, and this was the next item on the list. He would return a couple hours later and prepare for the next day's activities. Like a well-oiled machine, the hunt continued.

CHAPTER 17

"Nick, are you awake? Nick?" It was Fossum who woke him up.

"Ya, what?"

"Explain to me what you mean by thinking outside the box. I mean, I get what that means, but what do you mean?"

"I mean do what they least expect. Obviously, you've been trained to think and act a certain way. They're using that against you and your team. On the streets, we called it looking at a problem with new eyes. The smart criminals are always doing what they want to right under your nose. They know how to hide in plain sight. We had to learn to go under the radar, to think in new ways, see things in new ways. It's hard to do. You don't realize how your whole life is set in patterns that you follow unconsciously. Break those patterns, is what I mean. Think outside the experience of your life. What would you do if you'd never had the training you had? How would you see this problem?"

Nõn listened quietly while Nick tried to explain what he meant.

Then the door opened. Jay entered the room, well rested, cleanly shaven and meticulously groomed, even in the jungle of the Darien Gap.

Nick said, "Dapper as ever, Jay. Tell me, do you count the squares of the toilet paper before you wipe your ass? I bet you do. No more than seven squares needed to wipe Jay's ass. Any more than seven wouldn't be tidy and neat. You need to loosen up a bit, man, take a walk on the wild side, next time count out eight or nine squares and then wipe your ass. Who knows what'll happen?"

Jay tried to ignore the comments Nick made; sometimes, though, he wondered, *How the hell could he possibly know that?* Jay had always counted squares and carefully folded his toilet paper. He tried not to think about what that meant. He just liked his life orderly, there was nothing wrong with that, was there?

Regardless, Jay continued, "Fossum and Green, your time is up."

Nick watched as the two men were wheeled out of the room and nodded to Fossum; a silent *good luck, give them hell* passed between them. And the door closed.

Nick started to speak, "Listen, when they come for us, we have to be alert, aware, we have to see everything, hear everything. Pay attention to every detail, no matter how small, question it. Why is this here? What does it mean? What isn't here, and should it be? How does this help them hunt us? Do you understand?"

Nõn nodded that she thought she understood, but how could you really change the way you think and understand the world?

Nick ran over every detail he could remember of the past couple of days, the smells, the sounds. Every little nuance of every conversation. He had been in conservation mode until now, it was time to ramp up. Time to kick into hyperawareness. It was exhausting to do, but it could be a useful trick. Once it began, it was hard to shut down. This hyperawareness could be lethal. His body could tolerate it for only so long, then he would break down. He would crash hard.

Nick's sweat changed, the scent of his stressed mental state filled the air of the room. Hours had passed, and there was no return by Jay. Apparently, Fossum had listened, and he was making his sponsor work for it. No easy kill there, Fossum had stones. Good! More time to prepare for him and Nõn.

When the door finally did open, Jay was less jovial and seemed a little bit stressed. He wasn't as carefree as he'd been in the morning.

Nick said, "Jay, you look disturbed, it shouldn't be that hard to count out eight or nine squares, you really need to loosen up, man."

Jay said nothing. The day had nearly been a disaster. Green had done exactly as he was expected. He was dispatched quickly. Fossum, however, had done nothing expected and nearly killed his sponsor. Somehow, he'd flanked the guide and the sponsor and snuck up behind them; if it weren't for the RFID trackers each of the trophies carried, he would have killed them both. Fortunately, Jay had been able to intercede, and he had to kill Fossum himself. The day had not gone by the numbers, as he'd planned. It was a bit disconcerting and unexpected.

Jay told the workers to wheel the final two out and noticed the smell that filled the room. "Jesus, Nick, you need a bath, too bad you don't have longer to live. We may just have to follow the smell to find you in the jungle, you stink."

Nick blew his breath in Jay's face. "More where that came from, big boy, I'm sure you and the carrot sucking fat boy have been swapping bodily fluids while we've been sleeping. Tell the truth, is he your type? Common law relationships can work, it's just between us girls. Does he swallow or spit?"

"Keep talking, old man, your time is up. Time to get on the truck."

The truck stopped, and they were dropped off. Dirty uniforms were dropped at their naked feet, logger boots, a canteen and a knife for each. As the workers reached in a bag for their maps of Camp Baroota, Nick saw the unmistakable design of a directional antennae. The worker removed the maps and dropped them at Nick and Nõn's feet.

"Seriously, Jay, this is it? No hug?"

"Laugh it up, funny man, my guess is I'll be seeing you very, very soon." Jay smirked and glared at Nick with a cold stare.

The truck drove off, leaving Nick and Nõn standing naked in one of the vegetation bare trails made by the truck's tires.

Nõn started to get dressed, hurriedly trying to get as much distance between her and the camp as she could. Water would be first priority, then…she noticed Nick hadn't moved.

Nick glared at the direction the truck had departed. A slight snarl crossed his lips, and he whispered under his breath, "Ante up, motherfucker, the game is on."

Turning to Nõn, he said, "I don't think Jay likes me very much, not sure why, but I just get this feeling he'd rather not hang out and drink a beer with me again. Do you get that vibe, or is it just me?"

Nõn said nothing. Nick's constant stupid jokes were getting on her nerves. Did the man ever shut up? They were being hunted! She was nearly dressed and ready to get underway. She hoped to be a couple of miles from the camp in a few short minutes, if possible.

"Nõn, what's the hurry? Slow down, girl, no need to get dressed so quickly. Didn't you see what they had in that bag the maps came out of?"

Nõn didn't slow down. She had to get moving, now! Panic was setting in.

Nick grabbed her shoulders. "Nõn! Nõn! Stop. Stop it. Think."

"Getting dressed, that's what I am doing, let go of me, Nick."

"No, you're not, you're doing exactly what they expect you to do, what they hope you'll do!"

Nõn stopped. Nick was right; she'd already started to do exactly what was expected of her.

"What should we do then, Nick? Walk naked in the jungle?"

"No, what we should do is make sure there's nothing hidden in the seams of our clothing. When the driver reached into the bag to get out maps, I saw a directional antenna inside. Directional antennae are used for tracking animals that have been fitted with an RFID. A radio frequency identifier. Somewhere in all the gear they have given us is an RFID. Get those clothes off and start at the bottom and work your way up, feel for anything unusual. It could be a wire, or a small, pebble-sized microchip. When you're done, hand them to me, and I'll double check yours, you do the same for me. Funny that Jay quoted Sun Tzu at the bonfire the other night, do you remember that?"

Nõn nodded that she did remember. Nick continued.

"His quote was 'The supreme art of war is to subdue your enemy without fighting.' Do you remember?" Nick went on without waiting for Nõn to answer. "I thought that said a lot about the way Jay thinks. He likes to prepare, plan and have options for every contingency. It's mathematical the way he thinks. Funny, really, because normally it works A+B=C, it always works if you can frame the circumstances, you always win the game if you make the rules. Do you get it?"

Nõn replied, "Yes, I see what you mean, but the rules are the rules. How can you play and win when the rules are stacked against you?"

Nick smiled. "Exactly! You can't win, so you have to break the rules or change them. That's what we're going to do. Jay has made the rules, stacked the deck; we're going to un-stack it, change the rules."

The need to run was nearly undeniable, the anxiety overwhelming, but Nõn did as Nick asked. She kept focusing on the wolf on his chest as she felt the hem of her filthy pants. There was no denying what her dream meant now.

When they were done with the pants, they put them on. Nick started on his shirt, feeling the seams and bending the collar. Nõn started on her own shirt.

Nick continued, "Look at what Jay's done, he deprived us of water and now hands us a canteen each. What does that mean to you? What does that tell you? Jay suddenly wants us to get healthy? He cares about our welfare?

"These clothes, for example, why give them to us? Do we need them to run, to be hunted? No, but they serve some purpose for Jay's fucked up hunt, you can count on that. We just need to figure out that purpose and use it against him."

Nõn was starting to see what Jay meant, everything that had happened had been by design, Jay's design. Jay's plan. They could take nothing for granted, everything, no matter how small, had a purpose, a reason and existed for the hunt. Suddenly, she was scared. How can you possibly second guess everything? How do you know when it's part of the plan, and not just coincidence? She asked Nick exactly that.

He smiled. "Exactly. That's what makes the game, a game. However, now we have the advantage, Jay doesn't know what we know. He needs the deck to be stacked to win. Get it? We do the unexpected, change the rules, and he has to change as well. His structured world falls apart. We can beat him at his own game. But first we have to survive long enough to break his rules and set him on his heels."

Nõn was starting to get it. She looked at the knife and said, "Why give us a knife?"

Proudly, Nick said, "Exactly! Why? Ask what purpose does it serve Jay? Not how can I use it, instead ask how does he use it against me?"

They swapped shirts and started the process of searching over.

"Also, count on this. Jay will have layers upon layers to his rules. In case one fails, the next layer pops up. No one on the team has defeated all of Jay's rules. But I guarantee you, Fossum realized one of them existed and used it against Jay. He looked like someone stole his lunch money when he came back to the trophy room. He was really shaken. My guess is Fossum almost got away or maybe killed one of Jay's little helpers. Something happened to disturb Jay's structured little world. On the streets, I looked at it this way: there's always a feint within a feint within another feint, layer upon layer, you have to peel the onion to get to what's really going on. That's what we'll do to Jay and his little project, peel the onion, take his structured little world apart."

Nõn nodded; it made sense to her now. Talking about it calmed her. She realized her anxiety was less urgent.

Their shirts were cleared as good as they could be, so they passed them back and stood up to put them on. Nick turned around and looked down the single worn roadway they'd been driven on.

Nõn's eyes opened wide, and she yelled out to Nick, "Stop!"

Nick froze. The voice she'd used demanded his compliance. There was no question she meant exactly what she said.

"What? What is it?"

He felt her fingers between his shoulder blades, kneading the skin there. It was tender, and he winced. "What are you doing?"

Nõn said, "You have a small incision here, between the shoulder blades. I think maybe Jay has put trackers in each of us. What better way to track us than to plant the trackers in us? It feels like there is something small and hard under the skin."

"Get the knife they gave you, cut it out, now."

Nõn picked up the knife she'd been given and turned to Nick. "Ready?"

"Yes, hurry, we don't have a lot of time, we have to hurry."

A few moments later, Nõn knew she was right. She removed a small metallic cylinder from the fresh wound. It was the size of a standard pharmaceutical capsule.

She showed it to Nick, smiling.

Nick took the knife from her and said, "Now your turn. Take the shirt off." Nõn turned around and removed the shirt. There between her shoulder blades, hidden among the considerable scars, was a small red slit that had started to heal.

"Ready?"

"Yes, I am ready!"

Nick made a quick small cut and squeezed the area around the wound. The capsule erupted from the wound like puss from an angry zit. He nearly dropped it.

"Excellent observation, Nõn! Layer one of Jay's little hunting world just peeled back. Now we have to find the others."

They put the shirts back on and started on the boots they'd been given.

Finally, 10 minutes later they finished. They'd found no more trackers, but they knew more had to exist.

"Give me your canteen and knife."

Nõn gave him both, and Nick started to carve a huge semicircle in the dirt with the knives. He pierced both canteens and dropped them.

Nõn said, "What if they were not bugged? We could have used them; we will need water soon."

Nick ignored her. He placed the canteens side by side above the semicircle, then he stabbed the knives deep into the soil just under the canteens.

Nõn rolled her eyes. "Really, Nick, do the stupid jokes ever end?"

Nick had made a smile in the dirt. The eyes were the canteens and knives. He said, "Pull out your map, tell me what you don't see."

Pulling out her map, Nõn thought, *How can I see what is not there?*

She looked and looked. "I can't see what is not here, Nick! That makes no sense!"

Nick smiled. "Jay left out Baroota! The camp, it's not on the map; trees, hills, water sources, all there, but no Camp Baroota? Why?"

Nõn understood now what he meant.

"Tell me what you noticed when we left the camp, did you see anything weird or peculiar?"

Nõn thought long and hard. This way of seeing the world was exhausting, challenging every detail and questioning every object's purpose. She could think of nothing weird when they'd left the camp; they drove out of the gate and traveled down the road they'd been dropped on.

Nick smiled. "You see it, but you don't understand what it means. There's one way in and one way out. We'll have plenty of food and water soon enough, I promise you that. Drop the maps as well, leave them with the rest of Jay's gifts. We won't need them."

"Why won't we need them? I checked them both, there are no trackers on them, we can use them."

Nick quietly said, "Drop the maps now, and follow me."

He started walking down the roadway, still talking. He said, "Stay in the tire tracks, they drive in the same ruts over and over, their tires will destroy any of our own tracks, they'll have to hunt us old school style now, and we don't want to give them an edge."

Nõn hadn't followed him; she stood unmoving. "Nick, you are going the wrong way, we need to go that way!" she said, motioning towards the jungle. "That's the way out of here."

Nick turned to her. "No, we aren't going that way, that's what they

expect us to do. Death waits for us that way. We're going back to Baroota."

"WHAT?? No, I'm not! You're crazy, I am not going back there.
Look, the way out is that way. That's how we get out of here. Going back
to the camp is insane! Have you lost your mind?"

Nick stopped in the roadway. "Nõn, this is the direction they least
expect. No one in their right mind would go back to the camp. So you're
right, but that'll be the last place they'll look for us. I can't guarantee
we'll survive, but I do know this is exactly what they aren't expecting.
If you're determined to go that direction, I'll go with you. But I think
we'll regret it. It feels wrong to me. But I'll leave that up to you. Which
way, Nõn?"

Nõn looked down the road towards freedom, every rational thought
in her head said to go that way. She looked the other direction, just the
thought of returning to the death camp caused her anxiety. Back and
forth she looked, trying to decide what to do. Which was the right way?

Finally, she looked at Nick. Angry, she said, "No more stupid jokes,
let's go! I am hungry!"

Nick smiled. "Can't make that promise, girl. Stay in the tire ruts,
set the fastest pace you can hold, I'll follow your lead." They set off running towards Camp Baroota.

Nick said, "You know, I could be wrong, but think of the look on
Jay's face when he finds the smiley face cut in the roadway." Nick started
to laugh so hard, he stumbled and fell, gasping for air as he said, "God, I
wish I could see his face when he finds it. Where do you think he'll look
for us then? In the jungle, or in the camp?"

Nõn stopped and glared at him. "Come on, funny man. We have
to go now!"

Nick giggled and gasped for air as he climbed back to his feet and
started to run down the road.

In the jungle, a pair of curious brown eyes watched as the man and
woman spoke to each other in some kind of argument. Finally, they
turned and ran down the roadway towards the camp. Waiting a few
minutes, they followed and also went the direction of the camp.

Back in the camp, Jay was sitting in the command post. The technician there spoke up.

"Sir, they haven't moved since they were dropped off."

"Are you sure?"

"Yes, I'm sure. The signal is the best we've had on any of the group. They haven't left the drop-off site. They haven't moved at all. It looks like they just sat down and gave up."

Jay looked at the tracking screen. The tech was right; they hadn't moved.

"Give it a few more minutes. If they haven't moved in the direction of the water source, then I'll go out and kill them myself."

Jay left the camp a short while later in one of the trucks, speeding down the roadway towards the point where he'd dropped off the final two trophies.

Nick and Nõn heard a truck coming long before they saw it. The jungle was quiet, and sound carried easily and clearly. They had plenty of time to hide before the truck finally sped past. They could see Jay in the cab of the truck, along with one of the workers.

"Awesome!" Nick announced as they came from behind the foliage. "Do you realize what that means?"

Nõn, still breathing hard from their run, said, "No, what does it mean?"

"It means we got all the trackers; they drove past us, they didn't slow down, even a little bit. They can't track us anymore, we found all the trackers or left them there in the equipment."

Nõn realized it was true. It only made sense. Smiling, she said, "Let's go, before they come back."

They ran back to the tire ruts in the dirt road and sprinted towards Baroota.

In the jungle, a smaller pair of feet followed, staying carefully and quietly out of sight.

Once inside the camp, they slowed down and carefully moved from one point of concealment to another.

Nõn said, "What's the plan now? We are here, now what insanity do you have planned?"

Nick smirked. "Insanity? Me?" Laughing, he said, "You really aren't going to like this."

"I know I won't like it, I don't like any of this. Where are we going?"

"We're going to hide in plain sight, under the building with the antennae. Under their command post."

Eyes wide, Nõn thought, *Just like I believed, he really is insane.*

They ran from point to point in the camp, using the shadows in the afternoon sun to hide their movement as best they could. Finally, they arrived at the corner of the command post. There wasn't much room underneath; they had to force their way under the building, and once under it they found there was a little bit more space.

Nick whispered, "Now we wait for the right opportunity to turn the tables on Jay. Conserve your energy now, rest. When it's dark enough, I'll go out and scout the camp."

Jay arrived at the drop-off point and exited the vehicle quickly, ready for the ambush he expected, but never came. The whole day had been a pain in the ass. Nothing had gone according to plan, and now Nick was out here somewhere close by with Nõn. They were probably watching him now.

He scanned the jungle, looking for any sign of the two trophies. There was none.

Carefully, methodically, he slowly moved up the roadway, walking in the grass as he scanned the loose dirt for footprints. There were none.

Finally, he arrived at the point where Nick had left the canteens, knives and RFID trackers. The smug bastard had left him a message: a smiling face carved in the dirt. Nick and Nõn were in the wind, un-traceable.

Jay breathed a heavy sigh. He could call in the cavalry as a last re-sort. He motioned to the driver to get back in the truck as he picked up the equipment. No point in leaving it here. That would be a waste.

Jay told the driver to drive on to the kill site where they'd dropped off the two sponsors. They would need to be picked up and the plan changed. He couldn't leave them out here in the jungle with no way to know where Nick and Nõn were.

Had Nick and Nõn traveled down the road, away from the camp, they would have been dead already.

CHAPTER 18

Just as the sun set on the Darien Gap, Jay re turned with the two remaining hunters and their guide. They all got out of the vehicle and walked to the command post, Jay just ahead of the group. Once inside, Jay asked the technician if there were any signs of the two missing trophies, anything at all? The technician had nothing new to relay.

Nõn's sponsor was barely able to contain his rage. He'd anticipated killing the woman in the most violent method he could imagine. He had no intention of shooting her from a distance. He wasn't just interested in her death. He wanted her to feel incredible pain and suffering. He needed to hear her screams, smell her blood as it leaked from her wounds, wounds he'd looked forward to personally inflicting, slowly and mercilessly.

Kerry, meanwhile, was just happy to be back in the compound. The jungle was filled with insects that had found his baby soft and overly sensitive skin to their liking. In a word, he was being eaten alive by nearly every insect in the jungle. His arms and face were swollen from the numerous insect bites. He was miserable and whimpered as he touched the swollen welts covering his cheeks and surrounding his eyes. No one had told him not to slather his favorite perfumed lotion all over his arms and face when spending time in a tropical jungle. For the insects of the Darien Gap, it had been a pheromone-filled beacon calling them in for a feast.

Jay explained to the two men that the hunt would begin again in the morning, and he suggested to the two men to return to their rooms. They would need their rest if they wished to continue the hunt in the morning. They would have to actually find and kill their trophy. Their kills would take some skill and luck. The trophies would be out in the jungle the entire night and had a head start on them. He ended the speech with an attempt to sound confident. "Don't worry, gentlemen, we'll get you the kill you paid us for."

Nick and Nõn listened to the conversation between the sponsors and Jay from a mere 3 feet away. Lying facedown under the floor the men stood on, they might as well have been in the room with them. The sponsors left the command post, unhappy with the day's results but willing to try again tomorrow morning. Jay was relieved to have them out of his office. Once they'd left, he removed a hardened suitcase from a large sheet metal cabinet. Opening it, he removed the latest in night observation gear. It was fourth generation, military grade, with infrared heat sensing ability as well. If Nick and Nõn were anywhere hidden in the nighttime fauna of the jungle, the night vision gear would locate them. Jay prepared for a long night of tying up the loose ends of the final hunt planned for this mission at Camp Baroota. He told the command post technician he would return in the morning, at just before dawn, earlier if he was successful with the night vision gear.

Before he left the camp, Jay stopped into Fossum and Green's sponsor rooms and told them they would be leaving in the morning. He would escort them to the airfield and get them on their way. He congratulated Green's sponsor on the successful hunt and then apologized to Fossum's sponsor for the 'unfortunate incident', as he called it. Fossum's sponsor was just glad to have survived the incident and thanked him for saving his life. Jay left and walked to the now running truck with his driver waiting.

"Let's go find that asshole," Jay said as he got into the truck. Nick and Nõn heard the entire conversation about the night gear.

Nick whispered, "Time for me to scout our camp. Stay put, sleep if you can," and he silently crawled out of the crawlspace and disappeared into the night.

Nõn was nearly asleep when Nick returned. He smelled like he'd been standing in a campfire while it burned. The first thing he shoved into the command post's crawlspace were several bottles of water, then came the remains of an opened MRE he'd found in a garbage can near the trophy room.

"Enjoy, be back in a few," he whispered.

Nick didn't return for some time. Nõn drank one of the bottles of water and saved the rest for later. There was no guarantee of any re-supply. They had to conserve resources. She did eat the remainder of the MRE. Funny, she thought as she finished the thrown away food, she couldn't remember the last time anything tasted so good, much less someone else's garbage. When Nick finally did return, he could hardly contain himself. Crawling quietly back under the command post, he was in much better spirits.

"God, I love the dark," he whispered as he began to tell her what he'd found, done and planned. Before he could really get started, she said, "Nick, you smell like smoke, did you fall in the fire pit?"

"No, I crawled up to the fire pit and covered my face, arms and clothes with ash. I'm too shiny in the jungle heat; sweat reflects light, and the clothing they gave us is too light to effectively move around in the dark. It's simple camouflage, that's all."

Nõn nodded and listened as Nick continued.

"Jay has his favorite saying by Sun Tzu, let me tell you mine. There are many different versions of what Sun Tzu has said, but they all basically say the same thing in different ways. My favorite quote is something like this:

'The opportunity to secure ourselves against defeat lies in our own hands, but the opportunity of defeating the enemy is provided by the enemy himself.'

"Jay is about to get a reality check. While I was out, I found a gold mine." Nick was beside himself with the mischief he'd been into.

"On the first trip, I found the water and the MRE, and I thought that was probably as good as it would get. Jay has the place running like a well-oiled machine, but I think he's slipping. Yesterday's hunt with Fossum has really knocked him for a loop. He's made some critical mistakes, and now we can take advantage of them. First, he left the storage building where they put all of our stuff from the plane unlocked. 'The sponsors', as Jay likes to call them, get to pick and choose what souvenirs they want to keep, and then Jay destroys the rest. Anyway, I was able to get in the building and get some of our stuff back."

Smiling in the dark, Nick said, "Close your eyes, I have a surprise for you."

Nõn was suspicious as ever, but Nick insisted, "Go ahead, close your eyes and hold out your hand." Nõn looked at Nick for a moment and finally took a big breath, closed her eyes and then held out her hand. Nick placed something heavy and cold in her hand. "Now open them."

Nõn opened her eyes and could barely see the familiar object in her hand. She gasped and grabbed Nick by the neck and hugged him. "Thank you," she said over and over. Nick had found her knife.

"Shhhh…not so loud; there's still someone in the command post," Nick whispered. "I thought that might brighten your spirits a bit."

Nick continued, "So I went through all the stuff that's remaining from the last two kills. They haven't gotten rid of what's left, and guess what they have in Fossum's equipment?"

Nõn had no idea and said so, but Nick was having too much fun. "Come on, you can guess. Remember the briefing way back at Moses Hole?"

"Moses Hole? What are you talking about? Do you mean Moses Lake, the mission briefing with the flight crews and Jay and everyone?"

"Remember when I mentioned that back in the early 80s, I was actually stationed there when I was in the military? It was only for one summer, but it was a very long and hot summer. We gave the town the name Moses Hole, because there was nothing to do there and we were all bored beyond belief."

"Did Jay know you had been there before? I mean, did you mention it to him?"

"No, I never mentioned it; seemed like the less he knew, the better. I've always had issues with authority, and Jay instantly got on my nerves."

"So what else haven't you mentioned?"

"Nothing important! Anyway, you're changing the subject. Guess what I found in Fossum's gear?"

Nõn just waited as she continued to make eye contact with Nick; she knew there was no way he could keep the secret for long. Finally, he erupted, "OK, OK, you won't guess it anyway. He had Det Cord in his gear. Like 50 feet of it on a spool!"

"I don't know what Det Cord is, Nick, but from your excitement I can guess you think it is a very good thing."

"Oh, hell yes it's a good thing. It is like Christmas in July good, like Eva Mendes moved in next door and sunbathes nude good, like -"

Nõn impatiently interrupted him. "OK, OK, I get it, it is good, but why is it good?"

"Det Cord is an explosive, a really cool one. It can do all kinds of really cool stuff, but what's even better is that he has so much of it and the blasting caps to make it work. It's very stable and won't blow up un-less you have the right igniter, and now we have it, we have all of it! Jay is going to shit a brick when he sees what I have planned for his Camp Baroota!"

Nick's enthusiasm was starting to excite Nõn as well, and she said, "So what do we do now? What's next?"

"Next? Oh, nothing. Now we wait. I overheard the two remaining sponsors talking about leaving tomorrow and that Jay would be driving them. Guess Fossum nearly killed one of them and they want to get out of here ASAP. As soon as Jay returns, I need to borrow that knife and go back out into the night for a moment to do some underhanded dirty deeds, and then we relax for a while. We're still outgunned, and outnumbered. We just have some huge assets now in our favor!"

Nõn sighed; the man was fifty-four years old and still acted like he was twelve or thirteen. He was childlike and playful one moment, and deadly the next. An enigma wrapped in a mystery, that was Nick, she thought, as she gave him a dirty look and then let out a long, slow breath of air. He could be exhausting.

"Oh, and I found more food. Here." He handed her an unopened MRE, and she tore it open. They shared the meal silently while waiting for Jay's return.

The turn of events for Jay had continued after he went out in the jungle to look for Nick and Nõn. Once he actually got out of the truck and into the foliage, the insects had been relentless. Using the night scope had been a smart idea. It enabled him to view large areas clearly, and he was able to take up observation points on high hills and in trees that enabled him to increase his coverage. Problem was, they'd just dis-appeared. There was no sign of them. Zip, zero, nada. Finally, after sev-eral hours of searching, Jay decided to call it a night and come back in. Besides the insects feasting on his exposed skin, the batteries on the scope were dying quickly. The scope hadn't been used since the camp had opened for business, so the batteries weren't fully charged when he left the camp. He told the driver to pack it up, and he headed back ear-lier than he'd planned.

Nick had dozed off when he heard the truck returning to camp. He woke up and carefully felt his way around in the pitch dark of the crawlspace.

"Nõn, are you awake?"

"Yes, I am awake; it is hard to sleep with rocks digging into your back and bugs crawling all over you."

"OK, well Jay is back, so I need your knife. Can you hand it to me carefully? I can barely see anything, and I don't want to get stabbed."

"Reach your hand in my direction, and I will find it."

Nick reached out, and his hand touched her hair. Nõn jumped.

 "Sorry, that's me."

"It's OK. I am just a little jumpy from all the bugs."

Nõn took his hand and placed the handle of her knife in his hand. "What are you going to do with it?"

"A little preventative maintenance on those trucks. I'm guessing the oil hasn't been changed in a long time on either one. I just hate to see a fine piece of machinery like that abused."

"I hope you are joking," she said and then, "of course you are joking, you never stop joking."

Once Jay and the driver had stopped moving around and Nick was reasonably certain they were asleep, he crept out and crawled slowly to the parked trucks.

When he returned to the crawlspace, he smelled like motor oil. "There, that should do it. No matter what truck Jay takes tomorrow, he'll experience a delay and won't be able to return as planned. It might be a few days, if we're lucky."

"Are you going to share with me, or is this another secret that only you can know?"

"Don't be a hater, Nõn, of course I will share. It is perfect, really. I just made a small hole in the two oil filters of each truck. The oil will drip out slowly when they are parked, like they are now, but when the motor fires up, the oil system pressurizes and oil will come spraying out. Trucks that size carry a lot of oil in their motor, so by the time the engine runs out of oil and starts to really get damaged, Jay and company will be miles away from here. With any luck, the truck motor will be damaged beyond repair. Divide and conquer is the plan, my dear Nõn. Jay and one driver will be gone with the two sponsors. That leaves us with one driver here, the guy in the command post, and our two hunters. Time to turn the tables on them all."

"That is still four of them and two of us, Nick."

"Yes, it is. The hunters are going out to look for us in the morning, searching the jungles again. Their truck will run out of oil as well, so they may have to walk back. Unfortunately for them, we'll be here getting ready for their return. That leaves us to deal with just one guy, the tech guy in the command post. Poor bastard is about to have a very bad day."

"You are enjoying this way too much, Nick. I appreciate that you think through all of this, but it is a bit disconcerting as well to know this is probably what goes through your head all day, every day."

"No one really appreciates me," Nick replied sarcastically, "not even you. Sleep, Nõn, busy day tomorrow."

Nick then closed his eyes and went to sleep.

CHAPTER 19

Jay caught a short catnap and then was up preparing for the day's hunt. He scoured topographical maps of the area and tried to figure out where Nick and Nõn might have gone or hidden. He went to the room of both Green and Fossum's sponsors and woke them. He explained they'd each be able to choose whatever mementos they wished to take with them from the two deceased men's possessions, and then he'd accompany them to the airport. Leaving their rooms, he went to the small building where the men's final possessions had been stored. It wasn't comforting to find the building was unlocked. This wasn't acceptable. He was the only one with a key and had kept tight control over the access to the equipment from the very first hunt. He had to take responsibility for the slip of security. There was no other person who had access to the building. Jay entered the building and found nothing looked out of place from the previous hunts. He did notice a faint scent in the air that reminded him of smoke and thought it was strange.

The sponsors rifled through the dead men's possessions like shoppers looking through a bargain bin at Walmart on Black Friday, pulling out whatever items they wanted, casting aside those they didn't. Watching, Jay wanted the two sponsors to hurry up with the treasure hunt. He was impatient to get them driven to the airport and return for the hunt of the final two trophies. Jay could barely contain himself.

Finally, the two sponsors were finished and ready to go. Jay loaded their possessions in the truck while the two sponsors made their final preparations to leave. Jay made sure Nick and Nõn's sponsors were prepared for their hunt today. He had some final instructions for their driver/guide and then jumped in the truck and drove off as it started the two-hour trek to the Sambu airfield.

As Jay walked around the camp making preparations for the day's hunt and the trip to the airfield, Nick and Nõn watched from beneath the command post. Once the day's hunt began, they would be in the camp with only the technician. The odds would finally be in their favor.

Nick smiled and looked to Nõn. "I'd love to see Jay's face when that truck starts smoking. Poor guy's whole structured world is about to collapse from a few juvenile pranks. Imagine what that must feel like for a guy who prides himself on attention to details."

Finally, the second truck left the camp, taking the remaining sponsors out for their pointless hunt.

Nõn turned to Nick and said, "So what is next?"

"Time for the gloves to come off, Nõn. I'm not sure you really want to know what comes next. To be honest, I'd really prefer you weren't here to watch how dark this is going to get."

"I have seen evil, Nick, and I know these men are evil. I am just curious what is next."

"Next we have a little chat with the technician. But let's find some food first."

Inside the command post, the technician was waiting for the trucks to leave the camp as well. He was not only a mere technician for the camp; he was the director's eyes and ears inside the camp. A spy to keep an eye on the daily events at the camp. The director didn't rise to his position in life by leaving a program like the camp in a loyal underling's hands without some kind of secret intelligence gathering going on inside the program. His official eyes and ears about the camp's hunts and success came from Jay. The real story about the camp came unfiltered and raw from the technician inside the command post. Once the trucks had left the camp and the technician was sure he was alone, he relaxed a bit and opened the door to the command post. Stretching on the steps, he looked out on the jungle and listened to the sounds of the wildlife in the Darien Gap. Sitting down on the small metal porch, the technician pulled out the satellite phone that was his unfiltered connection to the director. Turning on the phone and waiting for the software to boot up and the satellite signal search to begin, he hoped the signal would be strong enough and last long enough to detail the situation on the ground.

Nick and Nõn were so close to the technician as he began talking to the director, they could have reached out and touched him.

As the technician began his conversation with the director, Jay was nearing the airfield. The vehicle was running rough and sounded like it was suddenly on its last tank of diesel. Jay was beside himself with anger. "What the hell else can go wrong on this hunt?" Pulling into the airfield parking lot, the truck's motor gave its final random belch of black smoke, shuddered, and seized. Metal bonding to metal, the truck would only move now under the power of another motor. The truck died a heroic mechanical death. Jay, however, was not impressed or grateful for its final efforts in getting them to the airfield. Jay was livid. Nick was right; if he could have seen the result this one juvenile prank had on Jay, he would have been elated. Jay's day was just getting started.

Back at the camp, Nick and Nõn listened as the technician detailed the difficulties of the week's hunt.

"Originally, sir, all had been well. The first day's hunts had set a new camp record, and the second hunt had also gone off without a hitch. The third hunt, however, had nearly been a disaster. One of the trophies had nearly killed a sponsor and the guide. Jay had to take matters into his own hands and kill the trophy himself.

Then the final hunt had been started the next morning. That hunt had totally come off the rails. The trophies were in the wind, their primary and secondary trackers had been removed, and no one had an explanation for how the trackers had been discovered. No one has ever discovered the trackers."

"And who are these final trophies?"

"The reporter and the old cop, sir."

A long silence, and then, "And what is today's plan?"

"Jay has taken the last successful sponsors to the airfield and should be returning soon. The last sponsors are out hunting the final trophies with their guides."

"All right, thank you for the update. Let me know any if any further developments occur."

"Yes, sir."

The technician hung up the phone and stood up. He turned and stepped up to enter the command post. Immediately, he fell; it felt like a hand had reached out and grabbed his foot at the last moment, but when he looked, he saw that his bootlace had just come untied. He had tripped on his own bootlaces. That's weird, he thought, rubbing the fresh bruise on his knees. The metal floor of the command post was unforgiving. The technician rubbed his knees and cried out loud, "Jesus, that hurts!"

Under the command post floor, Nõn was beside herself with anger.

"Really, did you have to untie his boot? Will you ever grow up? I swear, you are a hopelessly juvenile delinquent. That could have backfired horribly, and we could have been captured and killed."

Nick barely heard her as he tried desperately to contain his laughter. Soon enough, Nõn would wish the prankster Nick would return. The dark side of Nick was aching to be set loose on the camp.

They carefully crawled out of the crawlspace and stealthily scouted the camp, looking for food and water. They found one of the sponsors' rooms had been left open and entered. Inside, there was food and water, a shower, toilet, and some other minor creature comforts.

"Do you think we have time for a shower? I mean, I could really use a shower; I feel like bugs are still crawling on me," Nõn said hopefully.

"Sure, you shower; I'll keep an eye out. I have some stuff to do anyway."

While Nõn showered and discovered alarmingly she did indeed have several insects crawling on her, Nick broke out the Det Cord and began to plan for the day.

When Nõn returned, she found he'd made several loops of the Det Cord and set aside igniter caps for each loop. Looking in the room's closet, he found an extra large pair of sweat pants, a propane blowtorch, and a machete. "You're slipping, Jay; you're so slipping," Nick whispered to himself as he removed the sweatpants, blow torch and machete and put them on the bed with his supplies.

"I see you have been busy. If you like, there are extra towels and soap."

"No, I'll need a shower later. Trust me. Now's not the time for me to get all squeaky clean. Now's the time to get medieval."

The look on Nick's face was suddenly hard and distant. Nõn found it frighteningly similar to her childhood memories of the demon who now hunted her. A shudder erupted from deep within her shoulders.

"Last chance, Nõn. You can stay here. I'll come get you when it's over."

She just shook her head no. Silently, she knew she was in this, no matter where it ended up.

Nick took a long, deep breath and said, "All right then, let's begin."

The technician heard a set of footsteps coming up the two metal stairs and thought it was odd that he hadn't heard the return of the trucks. The door opened, and he started talking without turning to see who was there.

"So how was the airport, Jay? Everything go smooth as silk?"

"Very smooth," the strange voice replied. The technician, startled, stood up and turned quickly in time to see Nick, covered in ash and dirt, standing in the doorway of the command post.

"Mister, we're lost, can you help us find our mommies?" Nick said as he raised the machete he'd found in the room high above the technician's head.

Instinctively, the technician raised his own arms to protect his head from the pending assault. The machete cut through his right arm and severed it completely. The left arm absorbed the remaining energy from the strike, and the machete lodged into the meat and bone of the forearm. The technician screamed in agony and disbelief as he watched his severed right arm fall to the floor, lifelessly twitching.

"This was the quickest way I could think of to cure the pain from the fall earlier. Do your knees hurt now, my friend? No? No worries, I have just the thing to cure that little blood loss problem you're experiencing, and it'll help you forget about the pain of your newly missing arm."

Nick shoved the man back into his chair and tied him to it. "Now let's stop that blood loss; it's making a mess of this nice, clean and tidy office of yours." Nick lit the blowtorch and started cauterizing the fresh wounds.

Outside, the jungle erupted as flocks of birds quickly left the safety of perches high in the trees. The sound of an animal crying out as its final moments of life were horribly experienced disturbed them. They lived their own lives on the edge of death. To hear such an agonizingly horrible sound set them to flight, a reminder of what was possible at any moment. Whatever animal was in pain was close, much too close for the wildlife to feel safe.

When the man finally stopped screaming, Nick smiled. "There, now isn't that better? See how one pain makes you forget about another? Now, I have a little gift for you, it's a pretty little necklace of Det Cord. Do you know what Det Cord is?"

The technician was barely aware of the question and didn't answer. He just continued to gasp for air greedily, trying to make sense of the rapid change of events in his life. Moments ago, he was comfortable and sitting in his chair. Now, his body was writhing in unspeakable pain.

Nick continued, "No? Well, this necklace is much more fun than the pearl necklace you last received from Jay, on your knees, looking longingly into his eyes. This necklace shares some qualities with Jay's special gift to you, however; they both reach their climax in an explosion." Nick placed the Det Cord around the man's neck.

"Now that I have your attention, do you think you could fill in a few gaps for me? Like who is the director? Who's behind this little operation? Who really killed JFK?"

The technician was half-crazed and not understanding the joke as the pain rolled through his body, wave after wave. "Who killed JFK? How the hell would I know?"

"Funny that's all you heard," Nick said. "Do I need to relieve the pain you have in the other arm?"

"No, no, please, anything, I'll tell you anything!" The technician began to talk while Nick listened.

Nõn barely existed now in Nick's world. He'd warned her. She decided to stay the course of the wolf. Her dream had been clear. She would see this through, no matter how horrible it became.

"Now you just sit tight." Nick was satisfied he'd heard all the technician had to tell him. "I'll be back in good time, get some rest." Prying the machete from the man's nearly severed left arm, Nick picked up the satellite phone and walked out of the command post, closing the door, muffling the screams that rolled out of the tortured man. Once the screams had finally subsided, Nick flipped the switch on the electronic igniter and removed the troubled technician's head. The Det Cord necklace exploded, covering the inside of the command post with the fine mist of blood and brains, as it did what it was designed to do.

The sun had nearly set when the two hunters returned to the camp. They'd left in a truck accompanied by their driver/guide. The truck had broken down, and no one had the mechanical skill to know why. They'd been forced to walk back to the camp, and on the way back the demon saw something moving in the jungle, just in the shadows. Sprinting into the jungle, the demon wanted to kill something. The need to inflict pain on anything alive was overwhelming. He needed to hear the screams of an animal in pain. He'd hoped to wound a small deer or monkey, instead he returned from the jungle dragging a small boy who was fighting back as best he could. His resisting the demon only heightened the demon's sadistic need. The driver immediately recognized the boy as a child from his village; not just any child, but the Wounaan tribal leader's youngest son. The guide tried to stop the twisted man and save the child. There was no way, however, the demon would be denied, and the fat, soft man with them suddenly sparked to life and joined the demon in defeating his efforts to protect the child. There was nothing left to do but run to the village and hope he could get there fast enough to enable the tribal leader to save the boy.

The sight Nick and Nõn expected to see when the hunting trip returned to the camp was the three men walking exhausted from their day's unsuccessful adventures. They weren't prepared for the sight of the now beaten and bruised child being dragged by the demon, followed by the gleeful sexual predator, Kerry.

The men dragged the boy to a table near the center of the camp as the sun set and the jungle slowly began to darken. The child's helpless, frightened cries pierced the air of the jungle around Camp Baroota. The demon told Kerry to get a fire going while he restrained the child face down on a wooden table. Once he was restrained, the demon ripped off what little clothing the child had worn. The Wounaan people traditionally didn't wear much clothing in the warm Panamanian jungle.

Watching, Nick and Nõn were horrified. Nõn had been disturbed by Nick's behavior before the arrival of the demon; now she had to admit, she hoped he was just getting started.

Nick, watching the demon, spoke quietly, "Get the kid. Take your knife and cut him loose, get him to the jungle, don't come back. Just go, do you hear me? Don't come back."

Nõn nodded. Nick said nothing else and just started to walk towards the demon. Meanwhile, the demon was just getting warmed up with his sadistic torture of the child.

Nick broke into a sprint, approaching the demon silently from his blind side. He launched his body against the larger, younger man. The fight that erupted between the two men was brutal and feral; there were a few punches, but mostly the combat consisted of biting and scratching. Nick was too angry to fight intelligently. No part of his logical mind engaged the demon; this was a battle of instinct and emotions. In the rolling mixture of arms, legs, and dust, the primal battle continued. Nõn was startled by a pain-filled, enraged scream as Nick spit out the demon's left ear from his bloody mouth. She'd reached the child and freed him. She grabbed the child and began to run towards the jungle. The child barely understood that he'd been rescued; the terror he'd felt had pushed him into a state of fear that was uncontrollable. Suddenly, he was free and a woman was dragging him to the jungle, away from the men who had hurt him. As his fear subsided, he realized this was the woman he'd watched running on the roadway the day before. She had many scars on her body, he remembered, as her and the older man sat in the roadway talking. They slowly got dressed after handing each other their clothes back and forth. They were looking for something; he could see that. But nothing they did made sense. He was curious and followed them to the camp, watching as they climbed under one of the strange buildings. He had run home to the village and returned to the jungle today to continue to spy on the people there.

Once they reached the jungle, the boy came back to his senses and took the lead, pulling on Nõn's hand, as he was now in familiar territory.

Back at the camp, the fight continued. Nick was tiring fast. He hadn't been sleeping in a pampered room, eating regular meals and drinking water. The week's events had drained his strength. He had very little energy left and knew when the fight began, it was a futile effort. He could hurt the demon, but he wouldn't defeat him. He just hoped to give Nõn and the boy a good head start. Quickly, the demon gained the upper hand, slamming Nick's head into the ground and instantly disorienting him. The demon called out to Kerry, "Here is your trophy, what shall we do with him?!"

Kerry was beside himself with twisted glee and clapped his hands joyfully. "Oh, oh, let me go get my camera, I want to get pictures of this."

The demon stayed on top of Nick, pinning him to the ground. "I am going to enjoy cutting you up in little pieces, old man, then I will find and torture that redheaded bitch. She will wish she had finished me years ago."

Nick smiled a tired smile. "But the hyena was hungry. I bet you kept him, just to smell your dick on his breath."

The demon slammed Nick's head into the ground again and spit on his face. "You will know what I felt like soon enough, only I think I will feed you your own cock before this is over."

Dazed, Nick replied, "Is this some kind of weird initiation? I think I changed my mind; I'd rather pledge another fraternity."

Nick was nearly unconscious when his face was covered by warm arterial spray. His eyes were suddenly filled with blood, and he spit the hot liquid from his mouth, coughing. Funny, he felt no pain; this wasn't what he thought it would be like to bleed to death. Surprised the weight of the demon was no longer there, he could feel his arms were free, and he started to wipe the blood from his eyes. When he finally was able to see what had happened, the scene wasn't what he expected.

Nõn had run into the jungle with the boy and then stopped. Nothing in her dream included leaving the wolf. Nothing in her own heart said this was how she wanted to end this lifelong battle with the demon. She stopped and kissed the small boy's head and motioned for him to go, then turned and went back to the camp, hoping it wasn't too late.

Nõn arrived at the camp as Kerry was running back to his room to retrieve the camera. The scene was surreal as she watched the man skipping like a child as he ran, clapping and smiling his creepy, brainless and evil smile. She shook her head and continued to where she'd last seen the men fighting.

Listening as she quietly snuck up behind the demon sitting astride Nick, she heard that even now, defeated, Nick was taunting the demon. She smiled, hearing his stupid jokes; she realized it wasn't too late.

Nõn stalked the demon and silently came up behind him as he was about to reply to Nick's fraternity comment. In one violent and lightning fast movement, she grabbed a handful of his hair with her left hand and cut his throat with her knife in her right. The violence and speed of the movement was so fierce, Nõn decapitated the demon with one swipe of the razor sharp knife. The demon was instantly transformed into a human fountain as his life blood erupted from the wound, spraying the area around Nick and covering his face and eyes.

Nick slowly got up, exhausted, continuing to wipe the blood from his face. Looking at Nõn, he realized she still held the head of the demon in her hand. Nick shook his head and began to laugh as he looked at the surprised look on the demon's now detached head.

"And you called me the Nokunna? Really?"

Nõn replied, simply and quietly, "Finish this." She tossed the demon's head into the growing fire.

Kerry returned, still skipping and smiling that insanely stupid smile he'd left with. The scene, however, had changed dramatically. He blinked, trying to make sense of what he was now looking at. Nick, covered with blood, was walking towards him, every bit the nightmare Kerry had feared. Somehow, the demon had been bested.

Nick grabbed the soft man by the hair and dragged him to the table, slamming his fat face into the table, knocking him unconscious.

When Kerry awoke to the unpleasant odor of smelling salts being waved under his nose, he was standing upright; the table had been turned on its end, and he'd been tied to it. He'd been stripped of his clothing and now wore a pair of large, baggy sweatpants. Each of the legs of the pants had been tied tightly with twine. As his vision cleared, he saw Nick standing in front of him; beside him was a large wire trap, which was boiling with rats.

Nick spoke, "Welcome, Kerry, to your final day on planet Earth."

Kerry whimpered helplessly.

Nick ignited the blowtorch and turned down the flame to an evil blue glow. "Let's begin, shall we?"

Nick approached Kerry and smiled. "I promise, this hurts me so much more than it will hurt you; did your mom ever tell you that, Kerry?"

Kerry said, "Please, no."

Nick said calmly, "Answer the question, did she ever say that to you?"

"Yes, yes, she did!"

"And was she telling the truth?"

Kerry didn't know what to answer, so finally he said, "What do you want me to say?"

"The truth, Kerry. That's what I want to hear, the truth."

Kerry said, "I don't know if it hurt her or not."

"OK, well tell me, does this hurt?" Nick took the blue flame to Kerry's right pinky finger. He kept it there until the finger was nothing but a black stub on the hand.

Nick was unaware of the screams that filled the jungle. He was exhausted and running on pure rage. "I don't know, Kerry; I think that hurt me a lot less than it hurt you. Maybe the other hand?" Nick bathed the left hand pinky finger in the blue purifying flame, keeping it in place until that finger too was reduced to a charred stub.

"Ya know, Kerry, a few years ago I was on a case where the parents of a young boy decided that their son wasn't taking his toilet training seriously enough. The mother held the boy while the father took a butane lighter to his penis. Dad stretched the little boy's penis out and burned it off. The boy screamed while his mom held him.

"As I worked the case, I thought to myself, what would I do to those parents if I had 24 hours alone with them? The ideas that came to mind made me question my sanity, believe me. I've thought about that case a lot since we met. What would I do to you, if I got the chance? Unfortunately for me, I'm restrained by the resources available in the camp. These are the most creative tortures I could come up with on short notice. I do apologize; you deserve much better."

Nick continued, "You probably haven't noticed the yellow cord around your neck. Am I right?"

Kerry looked down, barely able to focus on the cord around his neck. He could now see it. There was a yellow cord around his neck. He looked up at Nick, terrified.

"That is Det Cord. And the little thing at the end of it isn't a stylish bolo tie. I know you were hoping for something stylish, but it was the best I could do. It's an igniter, and when the igniter goes off, so does the Det Cord. The result is your head pops off like a huge, infected zit. How cool is that, Kerry? I mean, really, did you think this was how your day would end as you left the camp this morning? Surprises all around for everyone, huh?"

"Do you like animals, Kerry?"

Kerry didn't answer.

Immediately, Nick went to work on the ring finger of the right hand, bathing it in the blue flame. When he finished, he asked Kerry again, "Do you like animals?"

Kerry screamed, "Yes, yes, I love animals."

Nick's filthy, blood covered face broke out into a huge smile. "Good, that's good. Right now, I want to introduce you to some of the local mammals."

Nick picked up the trap filled with rats. He held the trap up level with Kerry's terrified face, looking at him. "Don't you think they look hungry? I don't think they're getting enough to eat in the jungle here. They seem anxious, and yes, I think hungry, very hungry."

Putting the trap down, he continued, "Anyway, if all goes according to plan, I think they'll get some tasty treats to eat soon enough."

Nick started to explain the relationship Nõn had with her sponsor. He explained exactly how she'd taken the demon's power by removing his weapon of choice against the children he victimized. "So here this beaten down little girl is feeding the man's hyena little pieces of his cock while he watches helplessly. I have to admit, Kerry, I was impressed by her creativity. And I thought to myself, what can I do to one up that? Is there anything? I mean, how do you top that? It was a thing of beauty."

Kerry shook his head over and over. "NO, NO."

Nick kept talking to Kerry, tormenting him. Meanwhile, Nõn noticed the jungle was suddenly and ominously silent, then she saw one by one people appear on the edges of the firelight. The Wounaan had arrived in the camp, melting into the firelight from the shadows of the jungle. The tribe had them surrounded. There was no stopping Nick now, she knew that. She said nothing and let him continue.

Nick picked up the trap and quickly poured the crazed rats into the front of the oversized sweats. Some of the rats escaped before Nick was able to secure the rope around the waist of the sweats, but not all.

Kerry screamed now with every breath. He screamed until his voice was gone and his vocal cords shredded, and still he tried to scream. Silent, pathetic sounds came from his throat. Kerry's face was now distorted and filled with what Nick hoped was unimaginable pain.

Nick loudly spoke to Kerry over his soundless screams, "Can you feel the fingers I burned off now? I bet you've forgotten all about them, am I right?"

Kerry writhed and moved back and forth, doing anything he could to stop the rats' razor sharp teeth from shredding his genitalia. The sweats were beginning to shimmer crimson red as they soaked up the excess blood draining during the rats' feast.

Nick sat down and crossed his legs and watched. Suddenly childlike, absorbing the scene in front of him.

Nõn went up and quietly sat next to him. Looking at him, she now knew her epiphany on the bus had been correct. He would never admit the origin of the rage that drove him to this mission. He'd understood her immediately. They shared a commonality she hadn't realized until this moment. He wasn't even aware of her as she sat next to him; he was fixed on the poetically horrific scene in front of him. This was a debt that had long needed to be paid, and Nick was finally collecting.

Quietly, he said, "I've waited a long time for this day."

She knew exactly what that felt like. The Wounaan would probably kill them both at any moment, but they'd both finally, forcefully ended the reign of the demons that had haunted them.

Finally, Kerry passed out, his sweats drenched in blood as the rats continued their feast. Nick picked up the battery operated switch for the igniter and flipped it. In a moment, Kerry's head was reduced to a mist of bone, blood, hair and brains. Covered in the bloody pulp of what had been Kerry's head, Nick turned to Nõn and said, "I think I'll take that shower now."

The Wounaan had seen enough and took Nick and Nõn from the camp by force. They motioned to them both to follow the tribe into the jungle, weapons at the ready, should they decide to not cooperate. Watching the decapitation of Kerry and the demon had changed their opinion of the two alleged loggers, but they were still suspicious of them. Once they returned to their own village, the driver/guide explained to the tribal leaders what he'd been told of the hunts and the two sponsors' actions towards the small boy. Then it was the child's turn to explain his abduction. Finally, the tribal leaders called for an interpreter from another village. There was a woman there who had been educated in the schools in Panama and spoke many languages. When she arrived, she began to interview Nõn.

CHAPTER 20

Jay returned to the camp the following afternoon. He had to secure another truck and find a mechanic to begin repairs on the damaged truck they'd taken to Sambu airfield.

When he and the driver approached the camp, they could see something was wrong. There were huge flocks of birds picking at what appeared to be two dead animals in the center of the camp. Once they actually arrived in the camp, the birds took off and left the obvious remains of two decapitated men.

Jay was beside himself with rage. Storming to the command post, he ripped open the door to demand an explanation from the technician. He stopped just short of entering the command post. The walls inside were covered with a fine mist of blood, brains and hair, the stench was unbelievable. The technician had been attacked by someone who had removed one of his arms and nearly severed the other. What had happened to his head, Jay couldn't determine, except it appeared to have exploded all over the command post. In just twenty-four hours, the order and precision of operations in the camp had unraveled. Jay was stunned and a little overwhelmed. What had happened? Who could have done this? And how?

Jay's first instinct was to clean up, then do damage control. He moved the three decapitated bodies to the wood chipper and ordered the driver to get the machinery running and dispose of the bodies.

It was clear the two sponsors had been killed. They'd been worried by the birds and rats, so it was now difficult to determine exactly what had happened. Much of their flesh had been removed. Jay saw that in the now cold fire was what appeared to be a head. Burned beyond recognition, he wasn't able to determine whose head it was. Once the bodies had been cleaned up and shredded in the wood chipper, Jay knew he had to come up with a cover story. He asked the driver to contact the tribal leaders and ask for a meeting, He still had to clean up the mess from the previous day's hunt. His cover story with them would be that the two loggers had somehow escaped his crews and that he was asking for the Wounaan's assistance in locating and killing the missing loggers. Once the camp was reasonably cleaned up, the driver took Jay in the new truck and drove to the Wounaan village to make the request.

Jay arrived at the village and began his customary traditional greeting for the tribal leaders. Once the formalities were over and customary greetings exchanged, he explained that two of the loggers he'd hunted for the Wounaan had escaped from the camp. They were most likely hiding in the jungle and posed a very serious threat to the villagers. He asked for their help in searching for and killing the two loggers.

The tribal leaders thanked him for his concern and warning about the two loggers. They promised to send out a party to scout for and remove the missing loggers. They asked for a description of the loggers they'd be hunting. Jay carefully described both Nõn and Nick and explained they were dangerous and resourceful. Additionally, they were both capable of being very deceitful and manipulative. If they were captured, they would most likely have a very different account of how they came to be in the jungles of the Darien Gap.

While Jay was speaking to the tribal leaders, another conversation was going on with his driver. He was being debriefed and told to accompany Jay back to the camp and provide information about what had happened. He explained that when they returned, the camp was in complete disarray, there were three dead bodies in the camp, all of which had been decapitated. Two of the bodies had been so chewed on by the animals of the jungle, it wasn't possible to determine what had happened or who they were, except for the technician in the command post. He had been partially dismembered. The tribal leaders he briefed wanted to know what Jay had done with the three bodies. The driver explained he'd been ordered to shred them in the chipper and that this was the standard process in the camp for disposing of bodies.

Jay left the Wounaan with the complete confidence that they would follow through with his request and search for and kill the loggers. They didn't tell him they already had the two in custody and had begun their own investigation into what was happening in the camp. Although Jay may have thought the tribe unsophisticated, they were not. They'd been dealing with arms traffickers and drug lords for decades and had a pretty good idea he was misleading them about the real nature of the two loggers' identity.

While Jay was schmoozing the tribal leaders, Nõn was speaking with the interpreter.

It was quite a long discussion. Nõn detailed the entire process Jay had used to lure the team, she, and Nick, into the jungles. She explained how they'd been drugged and stripped of all their clothing and then paraded in front of their sponsors. When she was asked about the motivation for her sponsor wanting her brought to the camp, she explained her childhood and his role in abusing many children as a human trafficker. This explanation deeply disturbed the interpreter, but she continued to ask Nõn questions. Once she felt certain she understood Nõn's part in the killing of the demon, and the circumstances of the young boy's escape, she started to question Nõn about Nick's role in the camp and the beheading and torture of Kerry. Nõn described what Nick had done and why as best she could and then suggested they speak to Nick for any further questions the tribe may have had.

Once they'd returned to the village, Nick had been given some food and a place to sleep. He was told not to try to escape, or the consequences would be severe and immediate. He took that to mean he would probably be killed. He did ask to be able to clean up, since he was still covered with the muck of what had been Kerry's head. He was escorted to a nearby stream and allowed to wash the grime and blood off under armed guard.

He hadn't seen Nõn in several days when finally they came to question him. After his questioning was finished, the tribal elders called them to a meeting.

The interpreter began the meeting speaking for the tribal elders. First they thanked Nõn for freeing the boy and getting him to safety. Then they explained their belief system had no tolerance for beating or harming children. This was a sin that would deny a person's soul entrance into where 'Ewandama' is, 'Ewandama' being their most cherished god.

The interpreter paused and then addressed Nõn. "In our culture, your visions and spirit guide would be the sign of someone who has the powers of a Jai and has learned to harness these powers to become a Shaman, however we do not allow women to be Shaman. This is new to us, to see a woman with such powers. You are welcome to stay here with the Wounaan, if you wish."

The meeting went on for several hours, with Nick and Nõn asking and answering several questions. The tribal leaders wanted the camp removed from their lands. Nick had a suggestion that would solve all of their problems.

The director was in his office when the call from the technician's satellite phone came in. He expected the technician to have an update on the last hunt and answered the phone.

"Do you have an update?"

The voice he heard was not the technician's; instead, it was the Wounaan interpreter.

"I speak for the tribal elders of the Wounaan people. Camp Baroota is on our lands and is now forever closed. We will allow the lone survivor who remains to leave our lands. Anyone who attempts to return to the camp will be killed. That is all."

The line went dead.

Back in the Darien Gap, Jay had cleaned up the camp and was on his way to the airport. The driver had been given instructions to take him to the Sambu airfield and ensure that he left the Wounaan lands. When Jay arrived at the airport, he called the director as well.

"Speak!"

"Sir, this is Jay, update on the final hunt. The sponsors were successful in locating the two remaining trophies, and they're on their way home. The camp is shut down until the next hunt."

"Anything else I need to know, Jay?"

"No, sir. The hunt went by the numbers, as usual. Looking forward to your next task order, sir."

"That's good news, Jay, good work. I will speak to you soon."

The director hung up and made another call. The time had come to cut ties with everyone involved with Baroota.

Nearing the Texas coastline in the Gulf of Mexico, Pat was drinking some kind of rum and mango mixture while she sat watching the boat captain fishing for swordfish.

His phone rang, and he smiled as he spoke to the director. The conversation was quick and precise. The boat captain hung up and smiled at Pat.

"My son, asking if he can borrow the boat when we return. Would you like another drink while I fish, madam?"

"Please, yes, they're amazing," replied Pat.

The captain took her glass and returned a short time later with another. Sipping the drink, Pat watched as the captain yelled out he had a fish on the line and started the long battle with the fish. Pat fell asleep as she watched, the glass falling out of her hand and spilling onto the deck of the boat.

When she next woke up, she found her hands tied. The captain was cleaning the fish he'd finally brought onto the boat and was dumping one bloody mass after another into the water around the boat.

He smiled and said, "Hello, sleepy head. I was hoping you'd wake up. The chum is sure to bring sharks, and I wanted you to see them."

Pat tried to move but couldn't. Somehow, she did not like the tone of the captain's voice; something was different, menacing.

Watching the water, the captain cried out, "Yes! Yes! They're here, come and look."

He went to Pat and picked her up, helping her walk to the boat's edge so she could watch the sharks feasting on the now lifeless swordfish's bloody intestines and organs.

Moments later, the immediate area around the boat was filled with sharks thrashing through the water, competing for the bloody remains.

Pat, drooling, was fascinated by the fierce display of the sharks' hunger. She was still heavily drugged and unable to concentrate.

The captain laughed and remarked, "Look at how hungry they are, let's see if we have anything else to feed them!" He smiled at Pat and shoved her into the crimson foam created by the sharks' urgent thrashing.

The captain watched while Pat attempted to keep her head above water, crying out to him to help her. He smiled and raised a glass of rum to her in a toast, waiting for the sharks to attack.

He didn't have to wait long. Pat was treading water as well as could be expected drugged, fully clothed, and hands still tied together. She had only a few moments before she'd drown. Violently, she was suddenly pulled under the water. She fought her way back to the surface. Her left foot had been removed in one clean bite by the Mako shark that had attacked her. Panic had set in, and Pat was screaming to the captain to help her when she was pulled under again.

The feeding frenzy was in full force now, as Pat never returned to the surface of the water.

The captain watched for several minutes, glad to finally have the foul woman off his boat. She'd been a very unwelcome guest on his boat. When the director had called and told him to dispose of her, he was elated.

He picked up the cellular phone and called the director to inform him the problem had been taken care of.

The boat's motor fired up as the captain pulled away, leaving the scene for the seabirds that had already started to land, searching for any remaining scraps.

CHAPTER 21

Two days after Pat had disappeared into the waters of the Gulf of Mexico, Nõn and Nick were escorted to the nearby village of El Real de Santa Maria by the Wounaan. It was the nearest village that had modern services. The interpreter for the tribal elders had made arrangements for them to stay with a friend for a few days while they decided what their next step would be. As far as the director knew, they'd been killed. Jay also believed the Wounaan had killed them. To the rest of the world, they'd perished in the faked plane crash staged by Pat and Jay after the team had been drugged. They'd officially been declared lost in the "crash" after one of the bodies of the flight crew had been found along with some of the faked C-130 wreckage.

They talked through many plans and agreed they had to be extremely careful who they contacted. They had no idea how deep Jay and the director's dark tentacles had ventured into their lives. Contacting anyone could bring them both to the attention of the director once again.

After several hours of brainstorming, Nõn quietly said, "I think I know someone who might be able to help us. She's the international correspondent for NPR and is assigned to Mexico and Central America."

"NPR? Really? You think NPR is going to be able to help us?"

"You might be surprised what they can do. They work within the system, but outside of it, if you understand the subtleties of what that means. I just need to get her number and call her. If she can help us, she will."

An hour later, Nõn had the number and was calling.

"Hello?"

"Carrie?"

"Yes, who am I speaking with?"

"It is Nõn, how are you?"

"Nõn? What? Is this some kind of sick prank? Nõn is dead. Who is this?"

"I'm Nõn, and I need your help, and I need you to keep me dead. I am in a bit of trouble, and I have nowhere else to turn."

"OK, tell me something only Nõn would know. Anything at all."

Nõn replied, "Are you sure you want me to do that?"

"Sure, impress me with your knowledge."

"You confided in me once after we had been drinking margaritas that you had been having an affair with your husband's secretary. You made me promise never to tell anyone, and you told me no one else knew about it."

"Holy shit! Nõn, it is you. What the hell happened? We were told you were on a plane that crashed in the Pacific Ocean and everyone was lost. What happened?"

"I will explain later, Listen to me, for now I am dead, and I need to remain that way. I have some powerful people who wanted me dead, and I would like for them to continue thinking I am. Do you understand?"

"Yes, so what can I do? Where are you?"

For the next two hours, the women talked. Nõn explained that she was not alone and that she was with the other person she could trust. He too had to remain dead. They needed transportation, passports and new identities. Could she do that?

"It will take some time. I have some contacts who may be able to pull that off. Let me see what I can do, can you give me a number to reach you at?"

"I'll call you, best to be careful until we know what we are up against."

"Agreed. I'm so glad you're alive, thank you for reaching out to me. Call me back in two hours, and I'll have an answer for you."

Two hours later, Nõn and Nick had a plan. It would take a few days for them to get back to the U.S., but it was now possible to get back home. Carrie had arranged for them to meet a contact in Central America who would provide them with American passports and identities. They just had to meet the contact in San Miguelito Panama. Once they had their new identities, they should be able to travel freely. Once they had their new identities, Nõn was to contact her for money and flight arrangements.

It seemed too easy to be real after the events of the past two weeks. However, the next day they arrived in San Miguelito and met with Carrie's contact. They had new passports and Virginia state driver's licenses complete with their photos within hours.

After they'd returned to their room at the interpreter friend's home, Nōn called Carrie to thank her for the identification.

Carrie had made flight arrangements to enable them to land in LAX the following day. Carrie had set up an international wire transfer of five thousand dollars to an account in Panama. She explained the SWIFT code for Panama was BAGEPAPA and the money would be waiting for Nōn at the Citibank located at Av 17B Nte, Panamá City, Panama. Once they had the money, they needed to get to the Tocumen International Airport. Their flight would be an eleven and a half hour long trip on United Airlines. She'd booked two economy seats under their new names on flight #717, which had one stop in Houston, Texas, and then went on to LAX. Carrie said she would meet them there.

When Nōn explained the itinerary that Carrie had set up, he was impressed.

"Jesus, she works for NPR? Really, this is some detailed planning in less than two days."

"Well, reporters have to work fast. Sometimes a story breaks, and it takes some logistical skill to be the first one there. She has had a lot of practice," Nōn explained with a sly smirk.

The following day, they picked up the money and then hailed a cab to the airport for the remaining twenty-kilometer drive to Tocumen International Airport. Nick looked out the window of the Chrysler Pacifica as the driver skillfully negotiated the chaotic Panamanian traffic. The city was remarkably clean and well maintained.

Nick thought to himself, *I could live here under different circumstances.*

Nōn cleared her throat and then hesitated; she was struggling with asking Nick a question, not really sure she wanted to know the answer. Finally, she spoke.

"I have to admit, I am a little bit curious what motivated you to come here on this mission. I get the impression that if the original mission would have been real and we actually found human traffickers, you would have slaughtered everyone we found holding the children. Am I correct?"

Nick thought about how to explain his motivation for participating in the mission. Finally, he just said, "Yes, you're correct."

"Why? What motivates you to be so angry towards these people?"

"What makes you think I need to be angry or motivated to harm them? Your question implies it's either/or. What if the answer is neither?"

"That makes no sense to me."

"There are some things you just don't want to know about me, Nõn, some things I tell no one. Why didn't you mention the scars that cover you from head to toe? My guess is you don't like talking about them, that every time you look in the mirror, those scars remind you that in some way you'll never be free from your demon. You're forever marked by the time you spent in his sadistic care. Bottom line is, we both have our scars, yours are just more visible. Trust me, mine are there."

"But for me, the one big difference is I didn't come here to kill anyone, I was forced into it. I came here to document and educate the rest of the world about the issue of human trafficking. You have a dark side that's difficult for me to comprehend. There were a few moments back there at the camp I found myself afraid of you. Seriously afraid."

Nick said nothing. Looking out the window at the city, he seemed lost in the majestic views of Panama. There was an uncomfortable silence in the taxi as they continued towards their destination. Finally, Nick uncomfortably cleared his throat and smiled an uneasy smile at Nõn.

"How about I tell you about a hypothetical situation that may have actually happened? I knew this guy once who had been raised in what might have been less than favorable circumstances. Most people who have lived under these conditions end up being different than the rest of us. They become famous or infamous, with names like Bundy, Gacy, Ramierez, and Wuornos. The media would have you believe they're animals, but they aren't. They just never had the process of becoming what they were interrupted. No one stopped the train wreck that their lives were, no one stepped in and derailed it. Do you know the name Ressler?"

"No, I know the other names, but not Ressler."

"Ressler was the guy who first formed the profiling unit for the

FBI. Cutting edge stuff at the time. Personally, I think a lot of what he did was just common sense. Anyway, our hypothetical guy studied a lot of his cases and read every book he wrote, looking for clues as to what made people like the Gacys and Bundys different. He wanted to know was there a process that derailed who they were becoming? Could it be stopped? He found out there was. The difference between their lives and the rest of us that have shit storms for a life is the people who came in and derailed it. They showed concern for the person who was off track and headed towards infamy. Coaches, teachers, anyone who made them realize there was another choice. They didn't have to hunt their own kind. They could choose to be something else."

Nick paused, wishing he'd just ignored her question, wishing he could rewind this conversation and come up with some smartass comment to defuse the tension in the car.

Meanwhile, Nõn said nothing, listening. The layers of who Nick really was were being slowly peeled back, and as frightening as it was, she somehow already knew and understood this, she just hadn't heard it verbalized in such a way.

Nick continued, "So there are many potential Gacys and Bundys out there, walking among the sheep. Nuclear weapons that have been disarmed, the warhead is still inside them, but the fuse has been turned off. Does that analogy make sense?"

Nick didn't wait for an answer. "In my profession, there's this really stupid saying that we're sheepdogs protecting the flock from the wolves. The sheep don't like the dogs or the wolves, and don't appreciate what the sheepdogs do. That bullshit is repeated over and over by the overweight, soft handed, candy ass crowd I worked with. I never understood it that way. To me and perhaps our hypothetical guy, it feels more like this, mixed in-between the wolves and the sheepdogs, there are some that are hybrids. Not wolf, not dog, and definitely not sheep. They fit nowhere. They understand the sheep dog thinks with a siege mentality, which is doomed to fail. Better to hunt the wolf, with a wolf. Rather than wait for the attack, become the attacker." Nick was finished with his explanation and looked at Nõn with his eyebrows raised. "Understand?"

"Sounds like a very difficult position to be in, one foot in many worlds. Understood by none of them. Sounds like your wolf is very isolated."

Nick said nothing and looked out the window. A few moments later, the cab pulled into the airport parking lot. Nõn got out and paid the driver. There was a lot to mull over in Nick's hypothetical answer. Two hours later, their plane began its flight to Houston, with Nõn beginning to understand Nick was much more a mystery now than ever.

They'd been on the plane about 30 minutes when a steward offered them both a beverage.

Nõn replied, "Yes, I would like a bottle of water."

Nick interrupted that request immediately. "What she meant was she'd like a rum and Coke, make that two, one for each of us." Nõn looked at him with a curious look. Nick replied, "Really? Another bottle of water on another plane? I don't think so!"

The steward raised his eyebrows but said nothing. Nõn said, "Yes, I believe I will have a rum and Coke."

Once they landed in Houston, the plane taxied to Gate E #11. Processing through TSA from an international flight was the first real test of their new identities. They passed the TSA checks with no difficulty. Once inside the terminal, Nick stopped and stared at the monitors. There on a monitor he saw a flight from Houston to Colorado Springs, Colorado. It was United flight #5970, in two and a half hours he could be just a few miles from home. The flight would have him landing at dusk in the springs. He could be home an hour later. Home!

Nick looked at Nõn and explained what he was thinking. He didn't want to go to LAX, he could be home, at his home, in a few hours.

"I live in a remote area, free from traffic and people, no one would expect us to be there. We could stay there indefinitely." He explained that he hadn't left home on the best of terms with his wife, but at the last moment, just before they'd left on the mission, she'd sent him a text message telling him, "Good luck and see you soon."

"I'm not going to LAX, Nõn. You can go on, I'm going home."

CHAPTER 22

For Nõn, the decision was easy. She purchased a smartphone from a kiosk in the airport, and once it was activated, she called Carrie. She explained they'd changed plans at the last minute, just to be safe. She would call her tonight when they'd settled in and explain. There was nothing to worry about, it was just a minor change in their itinerary. Carrie thanked her for the update and told her to be safe. She and Nick then each purchased a seat on flight #5970. Nick was noticeably relieved. This was the happiest she'd seen him since they'd met in what now seemed like several years ago. They'd lived a lifetime in the past two weeks.

While they waited for the flight, they stopped to eat at the 3rd Bar Oyster and Eating House in terminal B. Nick noticed they served wine and asked Nõn if she'd like a glass of wine. Nõn explained she rarely drank anything alcoholic; since being drugged as a child, she'd been particularly careful about anything that impaired her physically or mentally.

Nick shrugged. "OK, I'm having a glass. If you'd like, I can recommend a good one."

Nõn said no at first, but when Nick's wine arrived, she changed her mind and asked the waiter to bring her a glass as well. The waiter asked her for identification, and for a moment she stopped, with a blank stare at Nick.

"Show him your identification, I think it's in your back pocket," Nick said with an eyebrow raised.

Laughing, Nõn retrieved the driver's license and handed it to the waiter. After the waiter left to pour her wine, Nõn started to laugh.

"This is all happening so fast, I forgot we had driver's licenses! It has been a while since I was carded for anything. I just don't buy alcohol, so when he asked me for identification, I just forgot!"

They talked easily for the first time since they'd met, talking about what to do next and how to proceed.

The wine arrived, and Nick raised his glass. "A toast!"

Nōn raised her glass in return. "To Camp Baroota, may we never cross its dark gate again, ever! Toast!"

Once they arrived in the Colorado Springs Airport, Nick went to the baggage claim area to rent a car. A quick 20 minutes later, Nick and Nōn were headed south to Nick's mountain home. Once they arrived at the dirt road that led to the house, Nick stopped. The house was still two miles away, but he could see the porch lights were on, and he could hear music.

Surprised, Nōn asked, "You live here? Seriously?"

"Yes, seriously, but the front porch lights are on and I hear music. Who has a party when their husband dies? Let's park the car and walk in; this doesn't feel right."

Nōn disagreed. "Nick, don't be ridiculous, there has to be a good explanation for the lights and music."

Nick ignored her and parked the car. Getting out, he started to walk; quietly, he spoke to Nōn.

"You'll need to stay close, there are serious predators here. Mountain lions and bears are common."

Laughing, Nōn said, "Be serious, mountain lions and bears?"

"I'm very serious. You need to stay close and be quiet, sound carries for miles here. We're two miles from the house, and I can hear someone laughing. That means if we aren't quiet, they'll hear us as well. Whisper from now on."

Nōn realized Nick was right, and also his attitude had changed; he'd been lighthearted moments ago, now he was dark and angry. Angry Nick was back in a heartbeat.

"When we get to the fork in the road, we'll be going left. There's a trail we call 'the fire road'; it's rough and barely passable, but no one will be on it. It'll take us to the house by the most direct route."

As they approached the fork in the road, the moon just started to peek out over the tops of the mountains behind the house. It bathed the valley in an eerie soft white. Animals jumped out in the bush ahead of them, startled by the two people walking in the moonlit night.

More laughter erupted from the house ahead of them, and there were at least three voices Nick could make out talking animatedly from the well lit porch. Finally, about 50 yards from the house, Nick stopped, hidden in the trees. Nõn came up behind him and looked at the people drinking and laughing on the porch.

Neither of them said a word as they heard Jay's unmistakable voice saying, "Then he said to me, 'I guess that makes you the gay one!'"

JoAnn replied, "That sounds just like him, cocky, arrogant asshole! You don't know how hard it's been to stay here with him these past few months. Watching him train and shoot, trying to convince himself he actually could contribute. Jesus, it was hard not to laugh in his face knowing what it really was he was training for. I wish I could have seen his face when he realized what the real mission was."

There was Jay, sitting on Nick's front porch, telling Jessica and JoAnn the events of the last two weeks. This wasn't what Nick had expected, not once had it entered his mind that he'd been set up by his wife. That this entire time she knew exactly where he was headed and what he was heading into. Jay, JoAnn and Jessica all drinking wine and laughing on his front porch. Laughing as Jay told them about the team and how each one died, and how finally he (Jay) had killed Nick and Nõn and fed them into the chipper. The two women exchanged high-fives and laughed louder.

Jessica said, "We're rich! With the money we made from the hunt and the life insurance policy, we'll be rich."

All at once, they cried out, "We're rich!"

Nick was too stunned to speak. He couldn't move.

Nõn touched his arm. "Let's go, Nick. You've seen enough, let's go."

"Fuck that! I can kill him right now, gut his ass like he wanted to do to us."

The trio carried on laughing and drinking. Thinking back, Nick remembered Jay's comment in the bar. "He said, 'You're the odd man out,'" Nick said to Nõn as they stood in the trees. "I knew then it meant more than he admitted to. I could feel it." He continued, "She texted 'see you in two weeks.' That wasn't for me. I see that now, it was a mistake; she meant to send that to Jay."

Nõn pulled again on his arm. "Let's go, Nick. There's no point in staying here and listening. Please, let's go. I have a bad feeling about this. We need to go, now!"

Nõn coaxed Nick to turn away from the scene, and slowly they made their way back down the fire road. The laughing continued as the trio celebrated their deaths and the pending payout of the insurance money.

Walking finally on the dirt road, Nõn coaxed Nick to walk faster; the more distance they put between them and the party, the better she felt. The need to get away from hearing the laughter and talking was intense. Once they reached the car, Nick stopped and looked back at what had been his home. He was numb from the reality of what he had to face, she'd set him up! He could hear them laughing occasionally, and then in the distance he heard a strange buzz. It sounded like a small air-craft flying high above the valley. He looked but saw nothing, no flash-ing lights to indicate a plane traveling overhead. The sky was clear, and the moon provided more than enough light to search the skies for the aircraft. He could hear it, but he couldn't see it.

Two hundred miles away, in a shipping container painted with des-ert sand camouflage, a remote operator was piloting an RQ-1 Predator. The UAV had acquired its target using the FLIR sensor. The operator was awaiting orders from the director.

"Zeus to Sparrow 434, what's your status?"
"Sparrow 434, I have target in sight. Confirmed three HVI on site."
"Zeus copies target in sight. Lock on target."
"Sparrow 434 copies, target locked, master armed."
 "Zeus copies, prosecute target."
"Sparrow 434 copies, prosecute target, weapons away in 3, 2, 1.
    Rifle. Time on target, 15 seconds."
"Zeus copies."
"Sparrow 434 confirms target splashed."
"Zeus copies target splashed."

The director hung up the phone and smiled. He loved the preci-sion of the UAV strikes. Signature strikes had been a closely guarded secret in the war on terror, but the strikes had made his life so much easier. The area was rural, and the fire investigators inexperienced. No one would suspect a thing. A horrible accident had occurred, the house had a fifteen hundred gallon propane tank. Evidence would show the tank's regulator had malfunctioned and the house blew up.

Twenty-five thousand feet below, Nick searched the night sky for the plane. He had no idea it was a drone, preparing to tie up the final loose end in the Camp Baroota nightmare. The director had many such camps functioning worldwide. He wasn't going to let the sloppy work of one man undo all he'd worked so hard and carefully to build.

Jessica and JoAnn had just slowly eased carefully into soapy hot water in the three man Jacuzzi tub in the master suite of the mountain home. Jay would join them in a moment; he had one more phone call to make. The girls weren't waiting for him to get the party started as they started to kiss and caress each other under the steaming, hot soapy water. It would be the last kiss they shared.

Nick watched as the house exploded in a huge fireball. The entire valley below was suddenly bathed in a bright orange light. The ground shook beneath his feet. He and Nõn jumped into the car and sped away. They said nothing for several minutes, each hoping their car wouldn't be the next target.

Finally, several miles away, Nick turned to her and said, "Do you know who was our beneficiary if we both died?"

Nõn shook her head, she had no idea.

Nick smiled huge. "My kids! My kids get the money now, there's no way she had time to change the will so quickly. She's been too busy getting her party on to change that. Ain't karma a bitch? The kids will get twice what she would have!"

TEN HOURS LATER...

In the Tamerisk Restaurant in the sleepy town of Green River, Utah, Nick sat and looked out the window, watching the river slowly flow past. He and Nõn had arrived in the town 7 hours after barely escaping the director's closing of what he thought was the final loop in the bungled hunt at Camp Baroota. They hadn't spoken much during the drive. Most of the past two and a half weeks had been spent trying to get to this point, alive and back in the U.S.; neither had given much thought to what they would do once they were back. Since they were officially dead, declared so in the faked crash staged by Jay and Pat, they couldn't safely return to their previous lives. Nõn had worked hard to earn a reputation as a tough but fair freelance reporter. Nick had no real life to return to and had built his life around the mountain home that was now ash. Sitting in the booth, they tried to process the events of the past 17 days. Their entire lives, identities and careers had been closed, sealed, and found moot in a few short moments. There was no way back. None.

Finally, after the waitress had returned with their orders, Nick cleared his throat and spoke.

"As I see it, we have one option only, or at least I have only one option. In my short interview with the technician back at Camp Baroota, he told me the director has many camps located worldwide in remote locations like the Darien Gap. In other words, Baroota wasn't an anomaly. Baroota is just one of the director's deadly infrastructure of camps. As I see it, we're probably the only people in the world in a position to stop the director from continuing these hunts. I say we go after him, and bring down his twisted world. It'll take time, and a lot of work, but really what else can we do? Hide and hope no one sees us?"

Nõn replied, "What can we do? We are not trained in tactics, we have no money, and no resources. The man just blew up a house on American soil with what looked like to me to be a drone strike. Who has that kind of power? And how do you propose we defeat someone in that kind of a position?"

"Exactly, Nõn! You already realize who the director isn't. He isn't the guy at the local gas station, or the county librarian. He shows us where to look by analyzing what he's done. Not everyone has access to what the director has shown us. Remember back on the road to Camp Baroota, I explained to you how to look at this with new eyes? Analyze what does each piece of information mean? Where does it lead? We defeated this bastard and his entire team at Baroota, you and I are the only survivors. We are as much on his blindside as you were when you decapitated the demon. Did you feel so incompetent then? We build a case file just like in police work, process of elimination until all that's left is the director and us. Are you with me?"

Nõn thought silently, *This wolf has no choice but to hunt, it is what he was made to do, and I have no choice except to follow.* Nõn breathed deeply and sighed. "OK, where do we start?"

Six months later, an anonymous text came in simultaneously to Nick's childrens' phones. The message was simple, something he'd told them repeatedly from the time they were small children.

"Success is a habit, so is survival."

ABOUT THE AUTHOR

Zach Fortier was a police officer for over thirty years specializing in K-9, SWAT, gangs, domestic violence, and sex crimes as an investigator.

He has written five books about his life in police work. CurbChek won the bronze medal for True Crime in the 2013 Readers' Favorite International Book Awards. Street Creds and Curbchek Reload won a gold and silver medal respectively for True Crime in the 2014 Readers' Favorite International Book Awards.

His other works are Hero To Zero, which details the incredibly talented cops that he worked with that ended up going down in flames, some ended up in prison and one on the FBI's ten most wanted list. Landed on Black described the toxic culture of the police department and streets, ultimately leading to the realization that Zach has been afflicted with PTSD. I am Raymond Washington is the only authorized biography of the original founder of the Crips and has been awarded bronze medals in 2015 by both IPPY and Readers Favorite International book awards.

If you are looking for gritty, true crime stories, be sure to check out all of Zach Fortier's novels. Zach currently lives in the mountains of Colorado, with his wife Christina.